TWO GUYS DETECTIVE AGENCY

by STEPHANIE BOND

Even Victoria can't keep
a secret from us...

CHAPTER ONE

LINDA GUY SMITH carefully lifted her gun to take deadly aim at the intruder. With her heart pounding, she squared his torso in her sites and held her breath as she slowly squeezed the trigger.

The squirrel seemed more startled than injured as the stream of water toppled him from the bird feeder to the ground, but the effect was the same. Duly warned, he scampered away toward the Logans' house next door. Linda blew down the barrel of her plastic water pistol with the satisfaction of an expert marksman, but she knew her victory was short-lived. After the creature sampled the discount birdseed in Mrs. Logan's feeder that was devoid of delectable black sunflower seeds, he would be back.

"But I'll be ready for you, you little thief." She set her weapon on the open window sill and turned back to her next most pressing matter—preparing school lunches and breakfast among the towering clutter that was her kitchen.

She could no longer remember when she and Sullivan had started the renovations. It seemed as if the cabinet doors had always been off, the counters always covered with plastic, the floor always tiled with uneven sheets of plywood. Linda sighed as she turned Very Veggie sausage patties in a nonstick skillet crowded with scrambled eggs. From the looks of their negative bank balance this month, they wouldn't be moving forward with the repairs anytime soon. Her stomach rolled with an unease that had nothing to do with the peculiar smell of the breakfast "meat."

The *tap tap tap* of toenails sounded on the floor. Max was a retired (and tired) police bloodhound with boundless patience, as evidenced by the sparkling pink tiara he wore.

"You're going to get teased by the other neighborhood dogs," she offered.

He ignored her jab, stopping to stare up at the empty birdfeeder.

"You missed my laser sniper shot at the enemy. But I don't think we've seen the last of him."

Max whined, then walked over and dropped his dead weight to lie on her feet.

"You are going on a diet."

He rolled his big brown eyes to look up at her.

"Okay, *we* are going on a diet," she agreed, trying not to think about the boxes of dark chocolate-covered cherries in the freezer—third prize in a local chocolatier's slogan contest. *(Bon bons fix boo-boos.)* Freezing them had been her way of rationing to herself the candy that no one else in the house liked…it took a long honking time to eat a frozen chunk of chocolate. But just yesterday, she had discovered she could thaw an entire box in the microwave in about thirty seconds.

"I should join the women's walking group," she murmured, although the thought of race-walking through the neighborhood with that color-coordinated herd struck a chord of rebellion in her. *That isn't me.*

Oh, yes, it is, her subconscious whispered. *Face it, Linda—you're regular.*

"Mom!" her nine-year-old son Jarrod shouted from his room down the hall, accompanied by thumping and slamming. "I can't find my UK cap!"

"Check the hall closet," she called without looking up.

She studiously turned the veggie sausage patties, as if to prove she was exactly where she should be, doing exactly what she should be doing. Being a mother and a wife in a perfectly nice little neighborhood in an older section of Lexington, Kentucky. So she and Sullivan struggled financially—didn't everyone? So she didn't feel fulfilled every moment of every day—who did?

Even twenty-nine-year-old women who had chosen a path opposite hers—an education and a career—had occasional pangs for the road not taken… didn't they?

"Mom!" her five-year-old daughter Maggie shouted from her room down the hall. "Where's my pink tiara?"

Linda exchanged a glance with the bejeweled dog. "Maggie, call Max and he'll help you find it."

"Come, Max!"

The dog rolled off her feet and trotted away, tiara bouncing. Linda turned to make peanut butter and jelly sandwiches laid out in assembly-line fashion— two for Jarrod, one for Maggie, grape jelly for him, strawberry for her. Baby carrots in baggies. Juice boxes. Hand wipes.

"Mom!" Jarrod yelled. "Where's my UK jacket?"

She closed her eyes and counted to three. "It's probably with your cap in the closet, sweetie."

A minute later, he bounded into the kitchen wearing the blue and white jacket and hat bearing the University of Kentucky insignia, his overgrown feet landing hard. She turned and her indefinable frustration dissolved at the sight of him—he was all boy, his fair father made over, but with her green eyes and her affinity for puzzles and number games. He came over to the stove, suffered a kiss, and held out the comics section.

"It says there are six things different between these two pictures, but I can only find four."

"Which four?"

He pointed them out as he recited them. She glanced at the pictures and rattled off the other two.

He frowned, hating to be bested.

"You give up too soon," she chided, then handed him a loaded plate and removed his cap to hang it on the back of his chair. "Maggie! Time for breakfast—you're going to be late for the bus."

"She's primping," Jarrod muttered. "What else is new?"

Maggie appeared, with Max dutifully following behind. Linda blinked. If her son was a mixture of her and Sullivan, Maggie was a puzzling little alien of extreme girliness who tested Linda's parenting skills on a daily basis. This morning in addition to the glittery tiara, her dark-haired little beauty sported black and white polka dot leggings, a yellow and orange flowered shirt, and a pink netting tutu around her chubby waist. But her mismatched outfit paled in comparison to the bright red lipstick that circled her mouth like clown paint.

Jarrod guffawed, but Maggie was unfazed as she climbed into a chair at the table.

"I look pretty," she said defiantly.

"That's quite an outfit," Linda agreed as she set a plate of food in front of her youngest. She'd committed to letting the budding fashion plate dress herself—the alternative left them both exhausted and teary.

Maggie made a face. "I don't want sausage. It'll give me cellulite." Linda was appalled until her daughter squinted and asked, "What's cellulite?"

"Nothing you have to worry about," Linda said pointedly. "Eat."

"It looks green," Maggie whined, prodding a patty with her fork.

"It's made without meat," Linda said. "It's good for you."

"You have to eat it," Jarrod said, shoveling in his food as if it were his last meal. "Mom won a year's supply."

For answering a trivia question in a call-in radio contest. Easy stuff.

"Where did you hear about cellulite?" she asked Maggie.

"On that dumb show *Beauty Pageant Diaries*," Jarrod offered. He drained his milk glass in one long guzzle, then wiped his mouth with his sleeve. "She watches it at the Logans' house."

"Use your napkin, please. And no more play dates at the Loganses." She lifted the corner of her apron to wipe off Maggie's lipstick under protest. "And stay out of my makeup kit."

Maggie pouted. "But Aunt Octavia sent it for your birthday and *you* never use it."

Linda caught sight of her reflection in a cracked mirror hanging over a bench piled high with power tools. Her blond hair was lank and listless, her complexion pale. The gray sweatshirt and faded jeans didn't do much for her, either. Maggie was right—she could use a little sprucing up. Why had she resisted using the luxurious gift her sister had sent? Because it represented everything she wasn't, and seemed to carry with it Octavia's ringing disapproval of her suburban-stay-at-home-mom lifestyle?

And stirred her own feelings of unrest?

Jarrod carried his empty plate to the sink. "Is the kitchen ever going to be finished?"

"Dad is doing the best he can," Linda said, although she was starting to wonder the same thing.

"Where *is* Daddy?" Maggie asked, still moving her food around.

"Yeah," Jarrod grumbled. "He was supposed to show me how to tie a knot for Scouts."

"He went into the office early. He's working on a big case. I can help you with the knot."

"I want Dad to help me," he said stubbornly. "I wish he'd go back to being a cop. That was cool."

A twinge barbed through her chest, partly to hear the disappointment in her son's voice, and partly because she herself missed Sullivan's former career—the regular paycheck most of all. But that was selfish of her. And now that he had almost a year under his belt at his own investigative agency, business would hopefully begin to pick up. "Being a P.I. is cool," she said in his defense.

"He works in a strip mall," Jarrod shot back.

"But there's a Waffle House next door," Maggie piped up. "That's *really* cool." She frowned down at the green sausage. "I wish I had a waffle right now."

"*Eat*," Linda said. "Mrs. Boyd will be here in a few minutes to walk you to the bus stop."

"I don't like Mrs. Boyd," Maggie said with her mouth full. "She says bad things about our house."

"Well, it's true our house doesn't look so great right now, but Daddy will work on it again as soon as he solves his big case."

Jarrod rolled his eyes. Linda felt obligated to give him a stern look even though she understood his sentiments.

The doorbell rang.

"Go get your book bags," she said needlessly as the kids went scrambling. She frowned suspiciously at Maggie's plate that was not only suddenly empty, but looked as if it had been *licked* clean. She leaned down to find Max lying under the table, staring up with innocent eyes, oblivious to the piece of scrambled egg on his muzzle that gave him away.

Linda sighed and turned to the counter to hurriedly stuff the lunch bags. She jogged to the tiny foyer, also cramped with displaced furniture and supplies from the ongoing construction, then pasted on a smile and swung open the door to greet her neighbor. "Good morning, Nan."

Nan Boyd was squeezed into a green workout suit in anticipation of the mid-morning neighborhood walk. Her face was fully made up, down to metallic eye shadow.

"Good morning," the chunky woman said, craning to see inside the house. "Oh, my, Linda, you're a *saint* to put up with these renovations for so long. If it were me, I'd have to put my foot down."

Linda gritted her teeth in the early spring chill. "Yes, well, Sullivan is really busy right now, but we'll get back to them soon."

"I hope so…for your sake, of course."

She turned her head. "Jarrod! Maggie!"

At the curb, next to where a clump of kids waited to be escorted to the bus stop, a brown delivery truck pulled up. The driver Eddie jumped down from his seat.

"Got another one for you, Mrs. Smith!"

"What is it, Eddie?"

He grinned. "A case of Kleenex."

Jarrod appeared at the door. "How did you win a bunch of Kleenex?"

She tweaked his ear and handed him his lunch bag. "By writing a greeting card verse to make people cry."

He shook his head and bounded down the steps, past the age of public kisses.

"Bye! I love you!" she said anyway.

"Goodbye, Mommy," Maggie said, lifting her cherubic face for a kiss.

Linda gave her a noisy sendoff, her heart squeezing. "Goodbye, sweetie. I love you."

Maggie took her lunch and skipped down the steps. Mrs. Boyd frowned after her, but was thwarted from making a comment about the bizarre outfit when she had to move to allow the driver to pass with the enormous box.

Linda waved and smiled. "Thank you, Nan."

Nan contorted to get in one last comment. "You should come walking with the other mothers sometime, Linda."

An invitation, or a threat? "I will," she promised, then turned away to hold the door for Eddie. Inside, she pushed and stacked items to clear a space for the prize.

"You always have interesting deliveries," Eddie said after he set down the box.

She laughed. "Surely you have something more interesting on your truck than a pallet of Kleenex."

"You'd think so, but no. What are you going to do with all that tissue?"

She shrugged. "Maybe I'll make paper carnations."

He grinned and extended a wireless device for her to sign.

With a stylus she wrote 'Linda Guy Smith.' She'd kept her maiden name as her middle name, a sore spot with Sullivan at the time—he was so traditional. She rarely used it, but was oddly compelled to write out her full name today.

The delivery was, after all, something she'd earned all on her own.

She walked Eddie to the door, glanced down the sidewalk for one last look at her kids as they moved en masse toward the bus stop, then stepped back inside and closed the door.

To heave a long pent up sigh.

She surveyed the clutter and debris and blinked back sudden tears, then foraged a dull kitchen knife to open the cardboard box.

One hundred forty-four cubes of pop-up Kleenex.

She removed one of the cubes and opened it, pulling out a fluffy white tissue to dab her eyes. How pathetic was it to be so proud of winning a gross of tissue? Truth be told, it wasn't even that useful. A pallet of toilet paper—now *that*, her household could've used.

The state of disrepair of her life seemed to be magnified this morning. She scarcely knew what to do first, doubtful if anything would make a dent in her to-do list, and knowing that larger issues were pressing down. Bypassing the dirty dishes, she moved into the tiny living room to reluctantly open Abby Guy's rosewood desk. How fitting that the one relic she had from her runaway mother would now be stuffed with other bits of her life that were so unsettling.

Blue on black.

An avalanche of unpaid bills sprang from every opening, spilling onto the floor.

Four hundred to the homeowner's association for monthly fees.

Six hundred to the hospital for the arm Jarrod had broken over six months ago.

Two thousand in late mortgage payments and fees.

And countless more thick envelopes that held equally ominous past due amounts—insurance, taxes, credit cards.

It had become the scary elephant in the house, this desk. Sullivan skirted it when he moved from room to room, his way of refusing to acknowledge its contents and what they meant to the security of this family.

She hugged herself as a slow burn rose in her stomach. Sullivan was a proud man, hadn't wanted her to work outside the home, but enough was enough. The kids were in school now and more independent. She hadn't finished her college degree, but she was teachable. She could do *something* to bring in some much-needed income, at least until his agency business picked up. Her family's survival was at stake, Sullivan's pride be damned.

With nervous excitement tingling in her belly, she scrounged a felt-tip marker from the desk and carried the jobs section of the *Lexington Herald-Leader* to the kitchen table. Max lay on her feet while she studied the classifieds one by one, waiting for something to inspire her.

Nothing did.

She quickly realized she was going to have to lower her expectations from the kind of job she'd like to have, to one that would have *her*.

On the second pass, she read more closely the more mundane service and retail positions that paid minimum wage. But even those jobs required experience, plus demanded hours that would interfere with her obligations at home.

A third pass was even more discouraging. At the end, she'd narrowed her options down to dog-walking, baby-sitting, and restocking vending machines. Resigned, she called the contact numbers for more information to apply, only to be told in every case that the job had already been filled. The vending machine company offered to put her on a waiting list. She shakily gave them her name and number, then disconnected the call.

A bubble of panic welled in her chest, vying with anger toward her husband. He'd assured her leaving the police force to start his own investigative agency was a good move, that it would give them more autonomy and he'd be able to spend more time with the family. Because he'd had a couple of close calls as a cop, she'd readily agreed, happy just to know he'd be safer. But only a few weeks after hanging his shingle, the economy had tanked, and the business he'd anticipated hadn't materialized. Now they were in debt over their heads.

She wiped at her eyes again, then blew her nose. When Sullivan got home this evening, she would make him sit down and admit they were in trouble, and together they would come up with a plan to dig themselves out. It would be good for them, good for their marriage. She was certain their looming debt was partly to blame for how distant he'd become over the past several months. Hadn't she come to their bed lately with her own unspoken resentments?

She steepled her hands and sighed. God help her, but more than once, she'd even fantasized about what it might be like *not* to be married to Sullivan. About starting over...

The cordless phone rang, jangling her raw nerves. She had the brief hope the vending machine company was calling her back, but that thought was dashed when she saw Lexington Division of Police on the caller ID. It wasn't uncommon for Sullivan's former colleagues to call.

"Hello?" she said.

"Linda? It's Oakley."

She smiled. Detective Oakley Hall was her husband's former partner on the force. He had been like family, and his absence was one of the reasons she missed Sullivan's old job. "Oakley, what a nice surprise. What are you doing with yourself these days?"

His silence sent dread arrowing to her stomach.

"Oakley?"

"Linda," he said, his voice anguished. "It's Sullivan. He collapsed at his office. I heard the call over my radio."

Her heart dropped to her knees, and her voice faltered. "Is…is he okay? Oakley, tell me he's okay!"

"He's on the way to St. Joe Hospital. I'm coming to pick you up. I'll be there in two minutes."

"I'll be ready," she murmured, and dropped the phone.

Ready. An odd choice of words considering she wasn't ready for this, wasn't ready for more upheaval in their lives. Linda stumbled around blindly to look for her purse, choking back sobs. Her mind reeled—what would she need to take with her? Her cell phone, wallet, insurance card—

A screaming siren announced Oakley's arrival. On the way to the front door, Linda grabbed the open box of Kleenex.

CHAPTER TWO

WHEN A PERSON is under extreme stress, Linda realized, the most mundane details are magnified. When Detective Oakley Hall, a bull of a man who wasn't yet thirty-five, emerged from his car to run around and open the passenger side door, she noticed he was starting to get a little silver in his sideburns and temples. And he must've dressed in a hurry this morning because his green and yellow paisley tie clashed horrifically with his blue and white striped dress shirt.

He and Maggie would make quite a colorful pair. She fought a hysterical laugh.

Oakley leveled his dark-eyed gaze on her and took her arm to help her into the seat. "Sully's going to be fine."

"Of course he is." The alternative was simply incomprehensible.

Oakley ran around the car and slid into the driver's seat, snapping his seatbelt into place and slamming his door in one motion. "Has he been ill?"

"Just a cold," she said cheerfully, gripping the box of Kleenex. "He's been working too hard, he's worn down." Her throat convulsed. "Was it his heart?"

"The EMT's were treating it as a heart attack, yes. But Sully is young and St. Joe's is a good hospital." He drove cautiously through the neighborhood. "I guess the kids are already at school?"

She nodded. "I'll have to go pick them up if…if Sullivan has to spend the night in the hospital and wants to see them."

"They're getting big, I'm sure."

"Yes."

"You look good."

"No, I don't...but thank you." When she'd first met Sullivan and his friend Oakley, they had both vied for her attention. But she'd been afraid of Oakley's bad boy reputation, had chosen Sullivan's happy-go-lucky charm instead. She turned her head and hated the worry she saw in his eyes. "Just get me there, Oakley."

He nodded, then turned his attention back to the road. At the mouth of the neighborhood, he turned on the siren and pushed the speed limit.

Linda forced complete emptiness into her head. She had a sense of landmarks passing as they left the Tates Creek area and traveled toward downtown, but little else registered until the hospital loomed in front of them. It was only then that her vital signs went haywire. Her own heart began to beat uncontrollably and she couldn't seem to get enough air. Oakley pulled the car into a spot for emergency vehicles and was at her door before she could release her seatbelt. His haste both reassured and frightened her, but she took his arm gratefully as he hustled her into the crowded emergency room waiting area and to the check-in counter.

"Sullivan Smith," he said, flashing his badge at the two women at the counter. "He was just brought in, presented with a heart attack."

One of the women moved to a computer screen. Suddenly Linda felt a touch to her arm. She turned to see Klo Calvert, an attractive woman in her mid-fifties, who was Sullivan's secretary at the agency. She'd been crying. Linda's breath rushed out as the woman clasped her hands.

"Oh, Linda—"

"What happened, Klo? Were you with him?"

Klo shook her head and teared up. "We didn't have any appointments. Sullivan told me to take the day off. Stone called me—he was with Sullivan."

Linda hadn't noticed the man standing nearby. He stepped up and nodded in greeting. She'd met Stone Calvert in passing. He was Klo's nephew who worked at the gym in the strip mall where the agency was located. Stone was a beefy guy, fortyish, with a shaved head. He'd spent some time in jail or prison, something like that—which explained the wary glance he gave Oakley. She recalled that Stone sometimes worked for Sullivan. Observing the man's bulk, it occurred to her he had probably provided muscle for Sullivan.

Had Sullivan *needed* a muscle man?

"What happened?" she asked Stone.

"I wasn't there when he collapsed," he said, his voice as gravelly as a state road. "He asked me to meet him this morning, and when I got there, I found him lying on the floor in his office. He couldn't speak, but he was conscious. I called 911."

"Thank you," she murmured and inadvertently reached out to touch his massive arm.

He seemed at a loss for words, so he simply nodded.

"Mr. Smith was just admitted," a woman behind the counter said, pulling Linda's attention back to the moment. "He's in ICU on the second floor."

Her breath rushed out in relief—he was alive. Still... "Intensive care? How is he?"

"Someone up there will be able to give you more details," the woman said gently, then pointed. "The elevator bays are down that hall. The waiting room on the second floor is more quiet than this one."

Once again, Oakley took the lead. Klo and Stone hesitated, but she motioned for them to come along. She made introductions and everyone shuffled awkwardly. No one wanted to be here. The elevators seemed to take forever to arrive, and the ride up was equally interminable. The hospital was surprisingly busy for so early in the day...so much sickness, so many tragedies, every day. It was the kind of thing people were oblivious to until it touched them.

When they reached the second floor, it took a few minutes to find the waiting room and longer to find someone to answer questions. A desk nurse scurried away to find a doctor and Oakley stayed with Linda.

She squeezed the Kleenex box, trying to stay calm. But her mind kept jumping around to other possible problems—had the payment for their health insurance made it by the cutoff date? Had the check cleared? Did Sullivan have disability insurance through the agency? And worse...why didn't she know? She hated she was even thinking about such things when she didn't yet know the extent of Sullivan's condition, but the financial implications had to be faced at some point. Panic licked at her stomach.

"Take a deep breath," Oakley said quietly. "Everything is going to be okay."

She nodded, breathing in and out…in and out. At that moment she was so grateful to have him there.

A tall woman wearing scrubs strode up. "Smith family?"

"Yes," Linda said. "How is my husband?"

"Stable," the physician, who introduced herself as Dr. Kozac, said. "But we still haven't been able to figure out what's wrong."

Linda frowned. "I thought it was his heart."

"It is, but some of his other organs have been compromised, too. Is he taking any prescription drugs?"

"No."

The doctor flicked her gaze to Oakley, then back. "Mrs. Smith, can I have a word with you in private?"

"You can speak freely. Oakley is my husband's best friend."

"Okay," the doctor said. "Does your husband take illegal drugs?"

Linda blinked. "No! No, of course not. He's a former police officer, he'd never do such a thing."

The doctor looked at Oakley for confirmation.

"To my knowledge, he's never taken illegal drugs," Oakley said.

Linda was irked with the doctor. "Why would you ask such a thing?"

"Just trying to eliminate some possibilities. Your husband hasn't been able to communicate with us. We're still running tests to find out why he collapsed."

"He's had a cold the past few days," Linda supplied. "But it didn't seem serious."

Dr. Kozac nodded to the box of Kleenex Linda held. "Is anyone else in the home sick?"

"No."

"Does he have any allergies?"

"None that I know of."

"Any history of family illness?"

"His father died of emphysema."

"Okay," the doctor said, although she obviously wasn't satisfied. "We'll keep you posted on his status."

"Can I see him?"

Dr. Kozac hesitated, then glanced at her watch. "A nurse will come to get you, but only you can go in, and only for a few minutes, at least until we know what we're dealing with." The doctor strode away, on to another emergency.

Linda looked at Oakley, fighting tears of frustration. "I still don't know anything."

"Let's go to the waiting room," he soothed. "We'll get a cup of coffee, and wait for word. He's in good hands."

She nodded, gripping the Kleenex box like a lifeline. Klo and Stone were in the waiting room. They stood, eager for an update. Linda shared what little she knew (leaving out the bit where the doctor had asked if her husband was a druggie), then settled into a stiff, worn chair. Oakley disappeared, presumably on the hunt for coffee.

She felt numb.

"I tried to reach you at home this morning," Klo offered, "but kept getting a fast busy signal."

Linda recalled dropping the phone after Oakley had called. She probably had compromised the system somehow. "Thank you anyway." She gave the woman's hand a squeeze, remembering her earlier comment that they hadn't had appointments today. Business was lousy, and she wondered if Sullivan had paid his secretary recently.

"I, um, couldn't get through to your cell either," Klo said carefully.

"It's probably turned off." Linda rummaged in her purse, debating whether to call Sullivan's widowed mother in Florida, or to wait until she had more news. She and Marbella Smith had never really gotten along—Linda sensed the woman still thought she'd gotten pregnant in college on purpose in order to ruin her son's life. Marbella had never considered the fact that Sullivan had been equally complicit in the unplanned pregnancy and that Linda's plans had been waylaid as well. That his mother had gotten two gorgeous grandchildren out of it hadn't seemed to matter—the woman was an iceberg.

Linda pulled out the cell phone and powered it up, only to see a message on the screen to please contact her carrier about her account. Translation: Her service had been cut off, which Klo probably suspected.

"Battery is dead," Linda mumbled, then stuffed the phone back into her purse. She felt sick...er.

"Use mine," Stone said, extending a phone with lots more bells and whistles than hers.

She smiled and thanked him, then stepped away to call Sullivan's mother. Thankfully, Marbella didn't answer. Linda left a brief message that Sullivan had collapsed and was in the hospital, but he was stable and she would call again as soon as she knew more.

She disconnected the call and wondered if she should call anyone else, but no names came to mind. Sullivan was an only child and was only casual friends with other men in their neighborhood. Besides Oakley, she couldn't think of anyone her husband would want her to call. As for her family, her father was... *indisposed*, so there was only Octavia, an hour away in Louisville. But married to a rich attorney, living in a gated community, and looking down her nose at her sister's life choices, Octavia might as well be a million miles away.

Linda realized she hadn't spoken to her sister since she'd called to thank her for the makeup kit a couple of months ago. The conversation had been fast and frosty and forced. She knew that for her sake, her sister would be sorry to hear that Sullivan was hospitalized, but suspected Octavia would somehow add it to the heap of shortcomings she attributed to the man Linda had married.

She walked back and handed the phone to Stone. "Thank you. You said Sullivan wanted you to meet him this morning?"

He was instantly on guard. "That's right."

"Do you know why?"

"I assume he needed help on a case."

She turned to Klo. "Would that be the big case he's been working on?"

Klo pursed her mouth. "I don't know...Sullivan has kept me a little out of the loop lately."

Stone wasn't the only employee of Sullivan's with a checkered past. Klo was a former stripper, and according to Sullivan, her network was extensive. He trusted the older woman; Linda sensed that he even relied on her. The fact that he wouldn't share details of a case with Klo was puzzling.

Oakley returned with a cardboard holder of large coffees to pass around. Linda drank deeply, welcoming the bitter burn and the zing of caffeine. It crossed her mind that she probably should be praying for Sullivan's recovery. Considering she hadn't been to church in a while, it seemed disingenuous to ask for a favor now, but she sent a request heavenward anyway.

"Mrs. Smith?"

She looked up to see a female nurse offering a tentative smile.

"I'll take you to see your husband now."

Linda handed her coffee to Oakley, who gave her a bolstering wink. Then she shifted her purse to her shoulder, curled the box of Kleenex in her elbow like a football, and followed the woman, her heart hammering in her chest. She was led down hallways, through massive swinging doors, and finally into a room lined with equipment that dwarfed the bed in which the patient lay.

She thought she had steeled herself for the worst, but the sight of her big, hardy husband lying listless and pale in a hospital gown was like a punch to her lungs. She gasped into her fingers, but held herself in check.

"Five minutes," the nurse murmured.

"Can I talk to him?"

"Of course. But he hasn't responded to anyone since he arrived."

The nurse left and pulled the door partially closed.

Linda approached Sullivan's bed slowly, choking back a sob as fear and apprehension invaded every cell of her body. She'd never seen her husband in a weakened state...he'd once pulled a double shift while suffering from the flu, and hit the winning run in a softball game with a broken rib. The beep of his heart monitor jarred her raw nerves. When anxiety threatened to engulf her, she took a deep breath and shook herself. Right now the most important thing was getting him back on the road to wellness.

Upon closer inspection, his freckled skin had a yellowish cast. His buzzed reddish hair was sweat-matted, his mouth slack. She used a Kleenex to dab the perspiration from his forehead. His eyes were closed and when she placed her hand on his cold fingers, he didn't respond to her touch. Her heart crunched when she realized someone had removed his ring. Neither of them had ever taken off their wedding bands.

She leaned over his bed to speak close to his ear. "Sullivan, it's me, sweetie. You're in the hospital, getting better, and I'm here with you."

No response.

"Sullivan, it's Linda. The doctors are trying to figure out what happened—"

His fingers moved beneath hers, and her heart gave a little jump of joy.

"I felt that...I know you can hear me." She squeezed his fingers again and waited for another response.

Instead, he made a mewling noise, as if he were trying to wake up. She pulled back to see his eyes fluttering open. He glanced around wildly.

Linda's shoulders sagged in relief. "Welcome back." She stroked his arm to soothe him, but instead, he grew more agitated.

"Relax, sweetie. I'm going to get the doctor."

But his fingers tightened around hers and his eyes pleaded. "Love...eee..." The sounds came out thick and distorted, as if he'd had a stroke.

She smiled. "I love you, too, sweetie."

But he shook his head, obviously distressed. Then his body went rigid and his eyes flew wide, glazed with pain. The heart monitor beeped in rapid succession, and another machine emitted an alarm.

Panicked, Linda raced to the door and yelled, "Help, somebody!"

The nurses were already jogging toward the room, with Dr. Kozac leading the charge. Linda was swept into the hallway, then handed off and shepherded back through the industrial swinging doors with the promise that someone would come for her as soon as he was stable again.

She raced back to the waiting room and when Oakley came to meet her, she sank against his chest. He calmed her with shushing noises and strokes to her back, as if she were a child, then led her to a chair. She told them what had happened in a halting voice. Another family had taken seats on the opposite side of the waiting room. A little girl stared at Linda and inched closer to her mother. It made her think of her own children, and how they would react to their father being so scarily ill.

"It's going to be okay," Oakley repeated over and over in that blanket-like voice of his. "Sully is strong and he has so much to live for."

Klo and Stone added comforting sentiments of their own.

She nodded and wiped, nodded and dabbed, until the tissue she held was shredded. In the melee of exiting Sullivan's room, she'd lost the stupid box of Kleenex. Oakley removed a snowy handkerchief from his back pocket and pushed it into her hand.

She blew her nose, feeling self-conscious about abusing such a personal item. "Don't you have to work today?"

He gave her a reassuring smile. "I'm not going anywhere."

Klo and Stone, too, stayed close. Linda made a mental note to tell Sullivan how supportive his friend and coworkers had been during the crisis.

There was so much she wanted to tell him, she realized, so many things she'd left unsaid recently because of trivial resentments. Her behavior now seemed so petty, she was ashamed. She would fix things between them, fix their family. They would be happy again.

They would.

After what seemed like an eternity, Dr. Kozac appeared at the doorway, looking weary—and holding the missing box of tissue. Linda surged to her feet and strode toward her, the others following behind.

"How is he?"

The doctor maintained a poker face. "Your husband suffered a massive heart attack and his heart stopped beating. We tried to revive him, but despite our best attempts..."

Everything shifted into slow motion as Linda recognized the "death talk" that was obviously required training for every physician. She braced for emotional Armageddon.

"...we couldn't save him. I'm sorry, Mrs. Smith." The doctor floundered, then handed Linda the dented box of Kleenex.

CHAPTER THREE

"POOR LINDA." Octavia Guy Habersham flipped down the visor mirror and smoothed her finger over the crease between her eyebrows she'd had filled yesterday with an injectable…again. It was the one area of her face that refused to respond to treatment. She checked her dark hair and her teeth, then flipped up the mirror and sat back. "What will she do now?"

From the driver seat of the Mercedes, her husband was quiet.

"Richard?"

He looked over. "Hm? Oh…she'll figure out something. Linda's a smart girl."

Octavia scoffed. "You couldn't prove it by her life choices. I'll never know why she married that clodhopper in the first place."

"I thought you said she was pregnant."

"She was, but she didn't have to *marry* the man. Now she has *two* rugrats, and no husband. And I doubt if Sullivan made any provisions for his death."

"Surely he had life insurance."

"When he was a police officer, maybe, but remember, he quit to become a private dick. What a joke. They're probably flat broke."

"You don't know that."

"Would you look at this?" She held up her right hand. "The polish on my pinkie nail is positively lumpy. It's impossible to find a good manicurist these days."

"It's like living in a third world country," he agreed.

"We have to help Linda out, you know. I'm all the family she has. Mother's gone and Father's…useless." She swallowed the bad taste in her mouth.

Richard pinched the bridge of his nose. "Has it occurred to you that you might offend her if you offer her money?"

Octavia gave a dismissive wave. "She'll have to swallow her pride. I won't let my nephew and niece grow up in squalor. Jarrod and Mary deserve better."

"I thought the little girl's name was Maggie."

"Maggie—right."

"Linda will be fine. She'll probably get a job." He arched an eyebrow. "Some women do that, you know."

Octavia sniffed. "You would hate it if I worked—who would take care of everything?"

"Gee, I don't know—maybe the maid or the cook or the gardener?"

"Very funny. I meant who would take care of our social life? Your firm has prospered because of all the contacts I've put in your path over the last few years."

"Yes, that's the only reason."

"You know what I mean." She pulled a checkbook out of her Gucci bag. "I'm going to offer her twenty thousand dollars."

"Twenty thousand?"

"More?"

"I was thinking less…if you want her to actually take it."

"Hm, maybe you're right. I can always give her more later, send her cash for the kids' birthdays, that kind of thing."

Richard loosened his tie, then leaned forward to turn up the air conditioner. "I was thinking we'd head back this afternoon after the funeral."

"No! I told you, I booked a room at the Marmot for the weekend. We're having massages tomorrow."

He pulled his hand down his face. "I really need to get back to the office, Octavia."

She leaned over and squeezed his shoulder. "Please? We're both so stressed out, it'll be good for us to get away for a couple of days. We can shop for a new watch for me." She glared, pressing down on her brow wrinkle. "I know Carla stole my watch."

"You made her take a polygraph, and she passed."

"You always take up for her." Octavia slid a suspicious look in his direction. Powerful men seemed to find that whole boss-servant thing pathetically irresistible.

"Carla is the most trustworthy person I know."

Hm. "How else could my watch have disappeared from my jewelry box?"

"You probably misplaced it, left it at the gym or something."

"I didn't, but regardless, I need a new watch and I don't want to wait for the insurance claim."

He sighed. "You can shop for a watch when you get back home."

Except she'd already talked to a jeweler on Nicholasville Road in Lexington who had the model of diamond Rolex she wanted—the only one of its kind in the state. "But I really should stick around Lexington for a couple of days to check on poor Linda."

He was quiet, but gave a curt nod.

She cooed and patted him on the thigh—a sign that if he got into a better humor over the weekend, he might get lucky...or a blow job, depending on how the syringe sites in her face felt tomorrow.

She wrote the check to her sister and tucked it back into her purse. "I just hope Linda takes this money in the spirit it's given."

Richard's phone rang. He cursed, then glanced at the screen and his mouth tightened.

"Ignore it," she said.

"I can't," he said in a weary voice. He put the phone to his ear. "This is Habersham...I can't really talk right now." He shifted in his seat. "That's not a good idea...no—" He looked at the phone.

"What happened? Who was that?"

"A client," he muttered. "The call dropped."

"You shouldn't be talking while you're driving anyway—what could be so important?"

"Will you be quiet!"

Octavia flinched—Richard had been in a snit for days, but he rarely raised his voice. "Excuse me?"

He sighed, then cracked his neck. "Sorry."

She angled her head. "You look a little gray—are you feeling okay?"

"I'm *fine*," he said with a chopping motion. "I just didn't get much sleep last night."

Actually, she'd noticed he'd left their bed in the wee hours to work in his office every night this week. "All the more reason to stay in Lexington this weekend," she sang. "We'll sleep in and have room service, those enormous strawberries—"

"I'm allergic to strawberries."

"—and maybe I'll splurge and have cream and real sugar in my coffee." She patted her flat stomach. "Javier has been putting me through extra cardio this month, so I can afford it."

"Speaking of, how much is the hotel room going to set us back?"

"Oh, we'll use points," she said with a wave. "We have a kajillion after we bought the Picasso on the credit card."

"Is this the exit?" he asked, pointing.

She looked up. "Yes."

When he slowed the car to pull onto the ramp leading into Lexington, it seemed to her as if everything else braked as well—life moved at a more leisurely pace in Lexington than in its more cosmopolitan sister, Louisville.

Octavia wrinkled her nose. She hated coming home.

Not that she'd visited Lexington lately. The last time she was in town for a Junior League event, Mary—er, make that *Maggie*—had been in diapers. And Sullivan and Linda had been doing renovations on their tiny little home in their shabby little neighborhood. A few minutes later when the Mercedes pulled up to the house, she realized nothing had changed—the neighborhood was still shabby, and the renovations were still underway.

"Is this it?" Richard asked.

"Unfortunately." She flashed back to the dilapidated little house she and Linda had grown up in. Hadn't her sister gotten a belly full of that life?

Since the driveway was jammed with minivans, Richard pulled into a spot on the curb.

"If you don't mind," he said, "I'm going to let you go in alone. I need to return that phone call."

"Okay," she said, opening the door to climb out next to a storage drain, then moved toward the driveway, her feet heavy in her black Christian Louboutin pumps.

Because of her background in cheerleading and beauty pageants, she shined at life's celebrations—birthday parties, weddings, anniversaries. Funerals, though, were sad, boring affairs where everyone's makeup ran. And she never knew the right thing to say.

But she lifted her chin and walked up to the front door of Linda's house. She would be there for her baby sister. She rang the doorbell and waited, hoping the inside of the house looked better than the outside. Just when she was about to ring the bell again, the door opened.

Octavia looked down to see a chubby little dark-haired girl wearing a tight pink flowered dress over a pair of red pants. The outfit was atrocious, but the tiara was a nice touch. The lipstick, however, was a little over the top.

"Who are you?" the little girl demanded.

Octavia frowned, holding her brow wrinkle. "I might be your Aunt Octavia. Who are you?"

"I'm Maggie. My daddy died."

Octavia's heart pinched. She didn't really connect with kids, but she crouched to look into blue eyes identical to her own. "I know. I'm sorry. I like your tiara."

Maggie dimpled. "I have more. Do you want to see them?"

Octavia nodded, and followed the little girl inside.

Sadly, the interior of the house was in worse disarray than the exterior. Tools and building supplies were stacked around the perimeter of the entryway and every room she could see into. People milled around, holding plates of food and talking in low voices. Rowdy kids chased each other. In the corner sat a mountain of Kleenex boxes—good God, had her sister become a hoarder?

She kept an eye out for Linda as she followed Maggie down a dim hallway into a tiny room that had exploded with stuffed animals and dolls, many of which were dressed in psychedelic clothing.

"Here they are," Maggie said, opening the middle drawer to a tiny white vanity with a perfectly proportioned mirror for a budding beauty queen. Her little round face glowed with awe as she looked over her sparkling toy crowns sitting on a green felt background.

Octavia knew just how she felt. "They're so pretty."

"I know," Maggie breathed. Then she looked up at Octavia. "My mommy won't stop crying."

Her heart twisted—and she had the urge to run. She hadn't told Linda she was coming…she could drop the check in the mail.

"Maggie, who are you talking to?"

Octavia looked up to see Linda standing in the doorway. She straightened. "Hi, sis."

Linda had sounded bleak on the phone, but Octavia was unprepared for how much her sister had changed since she'd last seen her. Linda had always been the prettier one, as fair as Octavia was dark, with a sweet disposition that lit her green eyes in a way no makeup could duplicate. But the woman standing before her was a faded flower, her bare face a study of devastation, wearing a too-long black dress and ugly flat shoes.

Linda opened her arms and Octavia went to her for a hug, but pulled back when the emotions started to overwhelm.

"Thank you for coming," Linda said, wiping her eyes with a tissue.

"Of course," she murmured. "Richard is here, too. He's parking the car."

Linda smiled through her tears. "There's quite a crowd here. I need to get ready for the funeral soon, and I'm not sure how to ask everyone to leave. They mean well, but…."

"Do what you need to do," Octavia said. "I've got this."

She retraced her steps to the living room and kitchen, wrinkled her nose at the array of sloppy, smelly dishes of food sitting on every horizontal surface, and tried to get the crowd's attention. When waving and pinging on a glass didn't work, she put two fingers in her mouth and produced an ear-piercing whistle that silenced everyone.

"Hello," she said with her best pageant smile. "I'm Octavia, Linda's sister, and we'd like to thank you for your support during this difficult time." She reached out and snagged a toddler by his collar as he ran by. "But I'm afraid I'm going to have to ask everyone to please collect their kidlets and their casseroles and leave."

They gawked at her, then at each other, then one by one, they began to move toward the door, gathering children and cake pans along the way. People talked behind their hands to each other, obviously put out with her eviction, but she didn't give a good damn what these rubes thought.

"Bye now…thank you…goodbye."

She stood at the door and ushered out the last guest, a chubby woman stuffed into a skirt, who seemed reluctant to leave. "I'm Linda's good friend Nan Boyd."

"Good for you," Octavia said. "Now, if you don't mind, this family needs some privacy."

The woman put her hands on her hips. "You don't have to be rude."

"Apparently, I do. *Goodbye*."

Nan Boyd's fat mouth twisted, but she turned and marched away. Octavia glanced to the curb where Richard was still in the car talking on his phone. She was shocked, though, to see his arms flailing and his face contorted. She'd never seen him behave that way when talking to a client.

"I remember you."

She turned to see a boy standing nearby with a hound dog sitting next to him. The dog wore a UK visor.

"I remember you, too, Jarrod." She closed the door.

"Where'd you learn to whistle like that?"

"My dad taught me," she said, then realized she'd said the exact wrong thing.

His eyes clouded over and he turned to flee down the hallway, presumably in the direction of his bedroom.

She closed her eyes briefly, then went in search of Linda, cringing over the disastrous state of the house. She sent a resentful barb to Sullivan that he would allow his wife to live like this. She wouldn't be caught dead living in this dump, and her sister deserved better, too.

Vaguely recalling the layout of the house, she walked to the end of the hallway past the kids' rooms and knocked on the closed door of the master bedroom.

"Come in," Linda called in a weak voice.

Octavia opened the door to find her sister sitting on an unmade bed. A pole had collapsed in the closet, whose door was off its hinges. Boxes of hardwood flooring were stacked against the wall.

"Everyone's gone," she offered.

"I heard," Linda said wryly. "I'm going to have to publish a blanket apology in the neighborhood newsletter."

Octavia scoffed. "Screw those vultures."

"Easy for you to say. I have to live here."

Her sister's resignation stoked her ire. "No, you *chose* to live here." But as soon as the words were out, she wanted them back.

Linda's mouth tightened. "And you look down on me for that."

Octavia sighed. "That came out wrong."

Linda pushed to her feet shakily. "No, it didn't. Why did you come, Octavia? To remind me I made all the wrong choices and look where it's got ten me?" Her eyes glittered with new tears.

"No," Octavia said carefully. "I came because I thought I could help you."

"Really?" Linda practically shouted. "My husband is *dead*, Octavia, and I have two kids who haven't shed a tear since I told them their dad isn't coming home, and I don't know what I'm going to do. How can you possibly help me?"

Octavia ached over her sister's palpable agony, while acknowledging her own inadequacy to offer comfort. She just wasn't made that way. So she opened her purse and removed the check she'd written. "Here."

CHAPTER FOUR

LINDA STARED at the check in her hand. "Ten thousand dollars?"

"There's more if you need it," Octavia said, her voice smug.

What she *needed* was to be able to tear the check into little pieces and toss them at her sister's designer shoes. But she couldn't...ten thousand dollars would catch her up on mortgage payments, utilities, insurance. Plus she'd yet to receive bills from the hospital and the funeral home. Still, her pride kicked in. "I can't take this," she said, extending the check.

"Of course you can," Octavia argued, folding her arms. "Don't suddenly stop being the sensible one."

Octavia had a talent for wrapping censure around a compliment. Linda hesitated, loath to take money from her arrogant sister, but knowing what it would mean for her children in the short term. "I'll pay you back," she said finally.

"Nonsense," Octavia said with a wave. "Now...what can I do to help you get ready?" She removed another item from her purse and held it up. "I brought waterproof mascara."

Linda smiled. That was Octavia—every problem in the world could be solved with money and makeup. But she was happy to submit to her sister's ministrations because she barely had the energy to dress herself, and she wanted to look nice for her husband's funeral.

Her husband's funeral.

The words were preposterous...incongruous...ridiculous.

Since the doctor's pronouncement, she'd been going through the motions of living. She couldn't stop—she had children to care for and a household to run and burial details to arrange. She'd made decisions no woman her age should ever have to make—this casket, those flowers, that gravesite.

If she'd hoped Sullivan's mother would help, she was mistaken. Upon hearing the devastating news, Marbella Smith had to be hospitalized herself. Her doctor had assured Linda over the phone her mother-in-law would recover, but was too fragile to travel for the memorial service. Linda had a hard time picturing Marbella as "fragile," but the woman had just lost her only child. Still, some part of her wondered if not coming to the funeral was Marbella's final act of disapproval of the life he'd chosen.

"There now," Octavia said, standing behind Linda in the bathroom mirror.

Linda stared at her reflection, impressed. Octavia knew how to work wonders with discount clothes, and the makeup kit had come in handy, even though most of the pots of color and stain had been violated by chubby finger pokes.

"Can I ask you a favor?" she said to Octavia.

"Sure."

"I'd like to go early to the funeral home to take care of some paperwork. Would you and Richard bring Maggie and Jarrod with you?"

She knew she was asking a lot because her sister had an aversion to little people. But to her credit, Octavia stiffened only slightly. "Of course."

"Thank you."

"Your little girl is quite the prima donna."

Linda bit back a smile. "Yes. She couldn't be more like you if she were *your* daughter."

Octavia sniffed. "I'll go help her pick out something more appropriate to wear than the blinding outfit she has on."

"Good luck."

Linda watched her slim, gorgeously put-together sister walk away, and squelched a pang of envy. Octavia had known what she wanted in life from a young age, and had set her sights on getting it. She'd parlayed her pageanting and cheerleading into enough scholarship money to attend the University of Kentucky where she had spurned the attention of any man who couldn't guarantee her the life she wanted. Richard Habersham had been a law student when Octavia had met him. With a family pedigree and preppy good looks, he'd fit her bill nicely. They were married the day after he graduated law school. (Only Linda knew that Octavia had secured wedding insurance in case Richard hadn't received his diploma as planned.) When Octavia had walked down the aisle, she'd never looked back.

By that time, Linda had dropped out of college. Her own wedding had taken place in front of the justice of the peace, and when she should have been graduating, she was juggling a toddler and learning how to coupon. The distance and the differences in their lives had driven a wedge between the sisters that had grown into a chasm over the years, especially since their mother was gone and their father had...spiraled out of control.

Linda sighed. She supposed she would have to get word to Nelson Guy sooner or later that his younger daughter was now a widow. She wasn't sure if he received the *Lexington Herald-Leader* at his current address of the Federal Correctional Institute in Manchester.

And the universe kept piling on.

Her limbs felt so heavy, she had to push herself to her feet. She felt a wall of grief bearing down on her, knew it would crash over her at some unexpected moment. She only hoped she'd have the strength to withstand the blow when it came. She'd done her part to keep the tsunami at bay—she'd opted for the lumpy futon in the extra room instead of sleeping alone in her and Sullivan's bed. She'd chosen not to bury her nose in the shirt he'd left hanging over the chair. She'd purposely not called his cell phone just to hear his recorded voice message. Her heart was like a plate glass window, utterly shattered, but hanging together by a thin covering.

Octavia's check lay on the bureau, made out in her sister's beautiful, curvy handwriting, the zeroes nice and round. The idea of having an extra ten thousand dollars lying around in a checking account was stunning to Linda. Next to the check was a framed photo of Sullivan in his police uniform. He seemed to be challenging her, telling her to thumb her nose at her sister's money, that she had everything she needed.

Except she didn't. She'd gone along with Sullivan's whim to change jobs, had trusted him to take care of them and now not only was she deeply in debt, but she didn't have Sullivan, either. And just this morning she'd gotten news from her insurance agent that Sullivan's life insurance policy, whose premium hadn't been paid in four months, would not be honored.

"You didn't leave me any choice," she murmured. "And now I have to go bury you."

She picked up the check, then gathered papers and other items she needed to take to the funeral parlor, shoving everything into a bag. She walked through the hallway, and stopped at Jarrod's door. She knocked, then waited a few seconds before pushing it open.

He was sitting on his bed, dressed in slacks and a dress shirt, tie, and his UK jacket.

She walked in and sat next to him, gathering him in a hug. "This is going to be the worst day of our lives," she said. "But we'll get through it, okay?"

He nodded against her neck. Still no tears.

"I need to go to the funeral home early to take care of some things. Will you ride with Aunt Octavia and Uncle Richard and keep an eye on Maggie for me?"

He nodded again.

"Okay, I'll see you there."

He hugged her tight and she let him hang on as long as he wanted to, but eventually he loosened his grip. "I'll take care of Maggie, and you, too."

Her heart twisted. "I know you will...you are your father's son."

She gave him a kiss, then went to see how Octavia was faring with Maggie. Not well, from the looks of the toe-to-toe standoff.

"I think you should wear the blue dress," Octavia said.

Maggie's dark eyebrows were drawn together. "I want to wear my tutu."

"You can't wear a tutu—it's not appropriate."

"What's 'propreate' mean?"

Linda stepped in.

Maggie lit up. "You look pretty, Mommy!"

"Thank you, sweetie. I think Aunt Octavia is right—your blue dress would look nice today."

Maggie's lip poked out. "But Daddy likes my tutu."

Linda bit down on the inside of her cheek. "You're right. But I happen to know he likes your blue dress, too."

Maggie brightened. "I can wear them both!"

"If that's what you want," Linda said, giving Octavia a pointed look. "Mommy's going ahead to the funeral home. You and Jarrod are coming with Aunt Octavia and Uncle Richard, okay?"

"I want to go with you," Maggie whined.

"Not this time," Linda said, shushing her. "Be good for Mommy, and make sure Jarrod behaves, too."

Having tattletale power over her brother cheered her up. "Okay, Mommy."

She gave her daughter a kiss and a hug, then gave Octavia directions to the funeral parlor. "Did Richard come in?"

"He's still in the car taking phone calls."

Linda said goodbye and made her way toward the garage. *Keep moving… keep moving and you don't have to think too much.* She stopped in the calamitous living room long enough to snag another box of Kleenex—she alone had made a good dent in the pile—gave Max a scratch, then exited to the garage, which was stacked so high with boxes of tile and two-by-fours, there was barely room for one vehicle. She climbed behind the wheel of the minivan cluttered with soccer equipment and turned over the engine.

Sullivan's leased car remained at the agency parking lot. Klo had confided they were so late on the payments, it would be better to just let it revert to the dealership.

The investigative agency was just another huge knot she would have to unravel.

But it would have to wait.

She backed out of the garage and down the driveway. As Octavia had indicated, Richard sat next to the curb in his big, gleaming Mercedes with his phone stuck to his head. A folder lay open on the steering wheel. His attention was so rapt he didn't notice her, and she decided not to disturb him. During the few times she'd spent in Richard's company, he'd always been nice enough to her, but she'd found him to have a chilly disposition. Still, he accommodated her sister's demands, which she knew were many, and the account the ten thousand dollar check was written on had his name on it, too, so....

She drove straight to an ATM to deposit said check, on the one hand feeling shameful to be tending to such tedious matters on the way to her husband's funeral, but on the other hand knowing her ability to write checks of her own today depended on it. When she pulled away, she conceded the relief of having money in the bank was immense. Octavia could be a witch, but she had to hand it to her sister for sizing up what she needed most at this moment.

She called her cell service provider and used the remaining credit limit on one charge card to have her service reinstated—another big relief, especially when so many people were trying to reach her right now. Sure enough, within a few minutes, her phone started beeping like crazy with undelivered voice messages. At traffic lights she paged through and discarded most of them, saving a few to return later.

We're so sorry to hear about Sullivan.

When her mind threatened to go to that place she couldn't bear to be, she turned up a radio station until the music was too loud to think. It worked until she pulled into the parking lot of the funeral parlor to see the name "Smith" on the marquee of the wood-framed sign.

Her husband was lying in there, his life over. There would be no more anniversaries, Christmases, or birthday parties. He wouldn't get to see his children grow up and have children of their own. They wouldn't get to travel and do the things they'd planned. Hell, he wouldn't even get to see the kitchen remodeled. She gripped the steering wheel so hard her knuckles cracked. It wasn't fair.

"It isn't fair!" she shouted. "It isn't fair! *It isn't fair!*" She screamed until her ears rang and her throat was raw and her palms hurt from pounding the steering wheel.

A rap on the window brought her up short. She turned her head to see Stone Calvert standing outside her van, his face a mask of concern. "Are you okay?"

Mortification bled through her. The man had witnessed a bona fide meltdown. Spent, she zoomed down the window. "No...but I'm better."

He gave her a tentative smile and she realized suddenly that he was a handsome man, especially when dressed in slacks and dress shirt. "I know this sounds trite, but you will be happy again someday."

She nodded, wondering if he spoke from experience…and thinking he was blowing his image of an ex-con by using words like "trite."

"The funeral isn't for another couple of hours," she offered.

"I know. Klo asked me to bring over some flowers the florist couldn't deliver in time."

"That's nice of you."

He looked pained, as if he didn't want to be thanked. "Mrs. Smith—"

"Linda."

"Linda…I was running a little late to meet Sullivan the day he died. I keep thinking if I'd gotten there sooner—"

"Mr. Calvert—"

"Stone."

"Stone…you can't blame yourself for my husband's death. His heart simply gave out. Thanks to you, he made it to the hospital, and he regained consciousness long enough to tell me he loved me. You don't know what that means to me."

The tension in his face and body eased somewhat. "Thank you for that."

She opened the door and climbed down. He gave an appreciative look at Octavia's handiwork, then seemed to remember himself. When she removed her bag of paperwork, he took it from her, and walked with her to the door of the funeral home. Next to his bulk, she felt positively diminutive.

When she took her bag, she thanked him again.

"Is there anything else I can do for you?"

"I'll have to rely on you and Klo to help me close the agency," she said. "But that will have to wait."

"Of course. Meanwhile, if I can do anything for you at your home…" His color rose. "I know Sullivan was doing some renovations. I'm good with my hands—er…that is, I'm handy."

She smiled. "I will definitely keep that offer in mind."

He nodded, then opened the door for her and said he would return later.

Inside the funeral parlor, she was assailed by the scent of death—mothballs and air freshener and live flowers. She wanted to turn and run...she didn't want to do this. Would it be so bad if she wasn't there for the funeral? People would just assume she was too grief stricken to endure the service, instead of the truth: That she was too *guilt-ridden* to endure the service.

She turned and had taken one step toward the door when an employee of the parlor appeared to greet her with cold hands. She followed him to the office where she signed a stack of papers, then wrote a check on a good portion of Octavia's gift as a down payment on the somewhat staggering invoice.

Dying was an expensive undertaking.

Soon after, people began arriving for the service—neighbors, teachers at the children's school, soccer parents, and members of the church they sometimes attended. Uniformed cops and other former coworkers of Sullivan's, including Oakley, who stayed close to her side. His presence was comforting, yet she sensed an undercurrent of tension between them in the way he wouldn't quite meet her eye. But she reminded herself that he was grieving as well.

Stone returned with Klo, who introduced her to two neighbors in the strip mall where the agency was located—Grim Hollister, a pony-tailed man who ran a pawn shop, and Maria Munoza, a pretty young woman who ran the dry cleaners. Linda greeted them warmly, but when she shook Maria's hand, the woman held on a few seconds longer, and held Linda's gaze with her coal black eyes.

"Sullivan didn't die in vain," she murmured with a faint accent.

Startled, Linda didn't know what to make of the woman's odd comment, until Klo leaned in. "She fancies herself a palm reader, don't pay her any mind."

Stone nodded in agreement, although she could tell he was affected by the woman's remark. Recalling their earlier conversation and the man's pressing guilt, she wanted to tell him to let it go, that her guilt trumped his. After all, while Sullivan had been lying on the floor, dying, she'd been home fantasizing about not being married to him anymore...about starting over.

And she'd gotten her wish.

The funeral director touched her arm. "Mrs. Smith...it's time."

CHAPTER FIVE

"I'VE BEEN THINKING," Octavia whispered to Richard as they were led to a pew near the front of the chapel to the tune of maudlin music.

"That's something new," he said dryly.

She ignored the jab—he'd been cranky the entire drive over. Between him and the kids—especially that mouthy little Maggie—she was ready to scream. "I think returning to Louisville after the funeral is a good idea."

"Why the change of heart? Too much family togetherness?"

"Something like that."

From his jacket pocket, his phone chimed.

"Will you turn that thing off?"

"Gotta take this. I'll wait for you in the car."

Irritated, she sat near the end of the pew, and set her bag next to her so she wouldn't have to share the space with someone. It was a packed house.

"Mind if I sit here?"

She looked up and tried to hide her disgust. Biker Man was tall and sinewy, his dark hair pulled into a ponytail. Tattoos spilled out from the long-sleeve shirt he wore onto his neck and his wrists. And someone needed to tell him that handle-bar mustaches went out of vogue two centuries ago. "Yes," she chirped, "I do mind."

"Guess you'll have to get over it," he said, then picked up her purse and dropped into the spot.

She suppressed an expletive and grabbed her bag—he looked like the type who could smell the jewelry case inside. Thug.

"Nice bracelet," he said, nodding to her diamond and onyx cuff.

She glared at him, pressing on her brow wrinkle—just as she thought.

"Grim Hollister," he said, introducing himself.

"I don't care," she returned with a saccharine smile.

In hindsight, she probably should've sat with Linda and the children in the front, but the detective who had been Sullivan's partner on the force seemed to have stepped in…hm. Neighbors and uniformed cops filled up the space between.

As expected, the service was a boring, sad affair. Octavia passed the time by inserting words of her own that the person giving the eulogy—the hunky detective again, hm—saw fit to leave out.

"Sullivan Aaron Smith was a good man."

Lazy.

"An ambitious man."

Self-indulgent.

"Who cherished his family."

So much so that he let them live in a construction zone.

"He leaves behind his wife Linda."

Who could've done so much better.

"And two wonderful children."

For whom he probably didn't even provide life insurance.

Throughout, her mind kept bouncing to Richard and she felt a little contrite. She nagged at him for working too hard, but he had always been a wonderful provider, and would never leave her in a lurch the way Sullivan had left Linda. She felt sorry for her sister, but she had made her bed, so to speak.

She scanned the faces of the seated crowd, passing over most, but stopping on one in particular.

Her breath left her lungs. *Dunk?*

Next to Louis Vuitton, Dunk Duncan had been the closest thing to the love of her life. When she was a cheerleader for UK, he had been a basketball star, which in this state, was akin to royalty. He had pursued her relentlessly, but Octavia knew better than to pair up with a man who was more high-maintenance than she was. She and Dunk both liked the spotlight, and when he was around, there was only room for him. He'd aged almost as well as she had, the handsome devil.

Why would Dunk Duncan be attending Sullivan's funeral?

Her chest clicked with nervous excitement even as she tried to force her attention back to the service. Mercifully, the funeral was short...ish. When the generic minister dismissed the crowd, she stepped over the Grim person and hurried down the aisle, keeping her eye on Dunk.

"Octavia? I thought you might be here."

She turned around to see a bespectacled, well-dressed man. Her memory chords pinged, but she couldn't place him.

"Oh, honey, don't tell me you don't recognize me."

And then the voice registered. "Emmett?"

He grinned. "Atta girl."

She grinned and hugged him. Emmett Kingsley had cheered with her in college. They'd been fast friends, but she hadn't seen him in years.

"How long has it been?" she asked.

"Only yesterday, because neither one of us has aged a day."

"True. What are you doing here?"

"I was hoping to see you. I heard about Sullivan's death and remembered he was your brother-in-law. I'm so sorry, by the way."

She gave a dismissive wave. "I barely knew him. What are you into?"

"I'm an events coordinator, which is how I know everything that happens in this town."

"I'm sure you're good at it."

"I am. Are you and Richard still in Louisville?"

"Yes. In fact, he's waiting for me in the car. We have to get back." She glanced to where she'd last seen Dunk, but he was gone. She felt deflated.

"We have to get together soon," Emmett said.

"Come to Louisville, we'll have lunch."

"I take it you don't visit Lexington much."

"No." She craned to look for Dunk—a man of his height should be easy to spot.

Emmett leaned in. "Did you see Dunk?"

Her attention snapped back, but she decided to play coy. "Dunk Duncan? He's here?"

"Yeah. He runs a swank investigative agency downtown—I guess Sullivan was his competition."

She snorted. "From what I hear, Sullivan's agency was in a strip mall and he kept company with questionable people." But Dunk was a P.I.? That was kind of sexy.

Emmett nodded over her shoulder. "I believe your family is waiting for you."

She glanced back to see Linda looking her way expectantly. "Yes, I'd better go."

He gave her his card. "Don't be a stranger."

She said goodbye, then made her way against the crowd back to the front of the chapel. She felt a tug on her dress and looked down to see Maggie.

"Careful, hon, this is Chanel. What is it?"

She pointed to the closed casket. "My daddy is in there asleep."

Octavia sighed and leaned down. "I know. You will miss your daddy so much." Although a parent dying didn't seem quite as hurtful as one walking out and never looking back. "But you have to be very strong and help your mommy not to cry."

"Do you have a little girl?"

"No."

"Why not?'

"Because I don't like children."

Maggie bit her lip. "I'm a children. Don't you like me?"

Octavia worked her mouth from side to side. "Maybe a little. You remind me of someone I used to know."

Maggie's eyes widened. "Who?"

"Me." She poked her in her chubby stomach and made her giggle. When she looked up, Linda was watching them. She straightened. "Sis...I'm sorry, but something came up and Richard needs to get back to Louisville."

Linda nodded. "It's fine. I understand."

She gave her a quick hug.

"Thank you for the money," Linda whispered.

"You're welcome," Octavia said, eager to get away. She loved her sister, but her situation seemed hopeless and she just wanted to put some distance between them. And see if she could catch Dunk before he left. She said good-bye to the kidlets, avoided the neighbors and the rest of the motley assembly, and exited to the lobby. She scanned for Dunk, but didn't see him in the waning crowd. Defeated, she walked out into the parking lot. Couldn't something go right today?

She stopped and looked around. That was strange—the Mercedes wasn't parked where it had been before.

Irritation sparked in her stomach. She pulled out her phone and texted *Where are you?* to Richard.

"Octavia? Oh, my goodness, I thought that was you."

She looked up and up and up into the handsome face of Dunk Duncan. Her body felt electrified, but her tongue remembered to play it cool. "I'm sorry, do we know each other?"

"We used to," he said smoothly. "I'm Dunk Duncan."

She feigned surprise. "Dunk! Of course! You look so...mature."

His jaw tightened, but he masked his annoyance that she hadn't acknowledged his preserved good looks. "You look the same, maybe better. Are you still in Louisville with what's-his-name?"

"Richard Habersham, and yes, I am. Richard was just named one of Louisville's top ten attorneys." She fixed an innocent expression. "What do you do?"

His chest puffed. "I have my own investigative firm."

"Ah. So you knew my brother-in-law?"

"In passing. I'm here out of professional courtesy. Unlike Sullivan, we only take on high-end cases."

"Oh? So there are dicks, and there are dicks?"

He pursed his mouth. "Something like that."

"And how's Tiffany?"

"Bethany?"

"Right."

"She's good."

But not great. Her phone buzzed.

"Do you need to get that?" he asked.

"Excuse me just a moment. It's probably my husband. He's so attentive."

She glanced at the screen, then squinted and read it again. *Things are bad, I have to disappear, need to sort things out. Stay with Linda for now.*

"Octavia? Are you okay?"

She looked up, could feel that her face was on fire. "I'm fine," she said, thoroughly exasperated with Richard and his long hours. But just because things were bad at the office didn't mean he was going to ditch her in Lexington. "I just need to call him back."

"Okay, well, it was really good to see you."

His gaze swept over her hungrily, and she felt her body loosen in response... dammit, he still affected her. "Good to see you too, Dunk."

As soon as he was out of earshot, she pressed the speed-dial button for Richard, and got his voice mail. She disconnected and tried again...and got his voice mail again. "Richard, I don't know what's going on," she seethed, "but you simply must call me at once!" She stabbed the End button, fuming. What had gotten into him?

"Octavia?"

She turned to see Linda standing in the door of the funeral home. "Can I speak to you for a minute?"

She tried to hide her irritation—her sister was having a bad day, too. "Sure."

Linda bit her lip as she approached. "I hate to bring this up, but the office manager just stopped me. I wrote a check against your check I deposited this morning."

"And?"

"And...I called my bank. There seems to be a problem with your check. It was returned."

Octavia scoffed. "It bounced? That's im—" She stopped as a horrible thought worked its way into her head. *Things are bad, I have to disappear.*

No...he couldn't...he wouldn't.

She walked out of earshot, pulled out her phone and called their accountant, threatening the receptionist's longevity if she didn't put her through *pronto.* She knew something was wrong as soon as Frank Bruno's voice came on the line.

"Octavia…hello."

"Frank, what the fuck is going on?"

He sighed. "I warned Richard this was going to happen."

"*What* was going to happen?"

"I...well..."

"Just tell me!"

He cleared his throat. "You're bankrupt."

A croaking laugh escaped her. "That's not possible."

"I'm sorry to be the bearer of bad news, but it's true."

"Frank, we have savings accounts...and investments...and a huge home!"

"Not anymore. Things have been bad for a while. I'm sorry."

Her vision dimmed. Richard's bad moods, long hours, and angry phone calls now made more sense. Ditto for all the calls from credit card companies, the ones Richard had told her to ignore.

"Where's my husband?" she whispered.

Frank sighed. "I was hoping you could tell me."

Her heart stalled in her chest.

"Octavia?"

She looked up to see Linda staring at her with concern.

"What's wrong?"

She'd been appalled by Linda's predicament—husbandless and broke... what modern woman allowed that to happen? It was simply unthinkable that she could be in the same boat.

And yet...she was.

CHAPTER SIX

"WHAT AM I going to do?"

Linda gripped the steering wheel and turned her head right to take in the sloppy, shuddering mess of her sister sprawled in the reclined passenger seat of the van. Remembering the waterproof mascara Octavia had given her, she thought her sister should've been so kind to herself. Her face was streaked black from hysterical tears, her red lipstick smeared past her nose, her dark hair standing up from Octavia literally pulling at it.

Linda was stunned—she'd never seen her sister display so much emotion. Octavia was the one who shrugged off unfortunate events as if they had no bearing on her. When their father had sat them down to tell them their mother had left on her own accord and wasn't coming back, her thirteen-year-old sister had stood and jammed her hands on her hips and declared, "Who needs her?" The next day her sister had announced she'd changed her name from Susan to Octavia, and told Linda there would be no further mention of their runaway mother. And that was that.

To see her sister so emotionally distraught was like seeing the sunrise at midnight—it went against the natural order of things. At a loss, Linda could only draw upon her maternal skills. "We'll figure it out."

Which only elicited another cry of dismay from Octavia and a renewed round of boo-hooing.

Linda pursed her mouth and decided that, like when Maggie was upset, it was best to just let Octavia wear herself out. She looked back to road and sighed. Leave it to Octavia to upstage her on the day of her husband's funeral.

Linda glanced in the rearview mirror at Jarrod and Maggie, who seemed transfixed by the adult tantrum in the front seat.

"Is Aunt Tavey upset about Daddy?" Maggie asked, her eyes wide.

"No," Jarrod said with a snort. "She's upset because her husband left her."

"Left her where?"

"With us," Jarrod said miserably.

Anger sparked in Linda's stomach that her children were being exposed to such a spectacle when they should be grieving for their father, but she allowed that for now it gave them all a welcome distraction. She suspected the situation wasn't as dire as Octavia portrayed it to be. Their accounts were most likely overdrawn due to Octavia's unbridled spending. Richard would probably come back for her when he had a chance to cool off.

Hopefully.

She tried not to think about the pickle the bounced check had left her in... she told herself she was no worse off financially than before Octavia had given her that money. And right now the canyon in her heart took priority. It was incomprehensible that she'd just sat through Sullivan's funeral...that he was never coming home.

That the world kept turning.

When she pulled into her driveway, the street was lined with parked cars full of people, waiting for them to arrive. Nan Boyd and others stood on the stoop holding Pyrex covered casserole dishes and Rubbermaid cake totes.

Octavia roused herself to snap, "Who are all these people?"

"Friends and neighbors," Linda said. "Armed with food and good intentions."

Octavia sniffed. "If they were your friends, they'd leave you the hell alone."

"They're only being nice," Linda chided. "It's expected that I let them in."

But she understood how Octavia felt. All those forlorn faces staring at her and tromping through her house, whispering about what might become of the young widow and her two children. She should eavesdrop, though, just to see if anyone had any insight.

She fumbled for the garage door opener and watched as the door rolled up to reveal more of their piled up clutter to their neighbors. But she was past the point of caring. She eased the van into the vacant spot that was barely big enough to hold the vehicle, then turned off the engine and hit the button to lower the door. She and the kids shimmied out and she was halfway to the door leading into the house before she realized Octavia wasn't with them.

"I'm staying here," Octavia said, laying her head back.

Linda saw the wisdom in her sister skipping the forlorn pleasantries and didn't try to change her mind. Octavia undoubtedly wanted privacy to take Richard's phone call when he eventually broke down and reached out to her. With any luck, all would be resolved by the time the last plate of macaroni salad had been consumed.

For her part, Linda pasted on a smile and opened her door to the flood of well-wishers, telling herself the gathering would at least postpone the inevitable loneliness that waited behind her bedroom door. She spent the next few hours floating from person to person, shaking sweaty hands and accepting stiff hugs and murmuring the same banal comments over and over.

Yes, Sullivan is in a better place. Yes, life is short. Yes, we'll be fine.

Bullshit, all of it, she thought while downing her third—or was it her fourth?—cup of bad coffee. Sullivan was not in a better place—he was across town lying in a cold grave in a hilly section of a rundown cemetery. And life was short only for some; the people who ran roughshod over others—her parents, for example—seemed to endure. And she was almost positive she and the kids were not going to be anywhere close to fine.

"What can I do?" came a familiar voice behind her.

She turned to see Oakley Hall, still in his dress uniform from the funeral, which she knew he'd worn out of respect for Sullivan, even though her husband was no longer on the force. His eyes were pained and pleading for her to give him a task.

Her heart surged with affection, then she glanced around at the hangers-on who seemed to have no intention of leaving, even as dusk fell. "Can you clear a room?"

He smiled and nodded. "Why don't you disappear with the kids, and I'll herd everyone out and lock up when I leave?"

She reached out to squeeze his hand. "Thank you."

"I'll call you tomorrow."

His words hovered around her like a security blanket. Accepting Oakley's help would be so easy. If any man could step into Sullivan's place, it would be Detective Oakley Hall, who would sacrifice himself to take care of his fallen friend's family. But no man *could* step into Sullivan's place—she owed her husband that much.

"I'm going to lie low for a while," she said. "I'll call you when I come up for air."

His mouth tightened, but he relented.

She turned and went in search of the children. Maggie was under a table with Max, tying bows in his ear fur. Jarrod was sitting on the couch holding his UK basketball and watching a sports show, ignoring all the commotion around him. Both children looked lost, and for a split second, Linda was furious with Sullivan for not taking better care of himself, for leaving his children fatherless. They didn't know yet what they had lost, but she did.

She clasped Maggie's hand and beckoned to Jarrod, then led them both to Jarrod's bedroom. Max trotted behind them, his head hanging low. Linda sat on the edge of the bed and pulled Maggie onto her lap. Jarrod refused to sit, began bouncing the ball on the floor.

Linda gritted her teeth against the unnerving noise that did little to help the headache hammering at her temples. "Uncle Oakley is going to say good-bye to everyone for us, so we can get ready for bed."

Thump, thump, thump went the ball. "He's not our uncle," Jarrod blurted.

He was already suspicious of a man trying to take this father's place—fair enough. "You're right," Linda conceded, "but he was like a brother to your father."

"I want to sleep with you, Mommy," Maggie said, snuggling closer.

"You're not a baby," Jarrod said, bouncing the ball harder.

"We can make an exception for tonight," Linda said, although she recognized it was as much for her as for Maggie. She wasn't looking forward to sleeping in her and Sullivan's bed alone.

Thump, thump, thump. "Then I'm going to sleep in the van," Jarrod announced.

"I don't think that's a good idea," Linda said.

"Why not?" he shot back.

"Because Aunt Tavey's going to sleep in the van," Maggie said.

"No one is sleeping in the van," Linda said firmly. Then she looked at Jarrod. "I want you here, in your room, in case Maggie or I need you."

Thump, thump, thump. Thump, thump, thump. "Okay," he agreed. Then he set down the ball.

A small victory, but she would take it.

"Are we going back to school tomorrow?" Maggie asked.

"I think that's a good idea if you want to." Linda extended her glance to Jarrod. "Or you can wait until Monday and see how you feel."

"Stacy Keller's mom is supposed to bring cupcakes for her birthday," Maggie said, clearly not wanting to miss out on the sugary fun.

"There's a ball game tomorrow between the fifth and sixth grade boys," Jarrod mumbled. "Coach said he might put me in."

It was a good sign that both kids wanted to get back to a normal routine—wasn't it? "Then I think you both should absolutely go to school tomorrow."

Maggie clapped her hands, and Jarrod looked somewhat relieved.

"Me and Max are going to brush our teeth," Maggie said, wriggling out of Linda's lap. She dashed out the door toward the bathroom, and Max loped after her, ribbons bouncing.

From the open door to the hallway, blessed silence sounded. She mentally thanked Oakley for getting rid of everyone, then pushed to her feet. "It's been a long, difficult day," she said to Jarrod. "Thank you for being so grown up and well-behaved."

He grunted and let her hug him, a rarity these days. He even hugged back for a few desperate seconds, then reeled away and went to pick up his basketball. *Thump, thump, thump.*

So much like his father—she would have to let him process everything in his own timeframe. "Why don't you get ready for bed and I'll be back to say goodnight."

When she got to the door, he said, "Mom?"

She turned back. "Yes, sweetie?"

He chewed his lower lip. "What are we going to do for money?"

Hearing her son's anguish knocked the wind from her lungs.

"I have almost thirty-two dollars in my bank," he offered, "and I can get a job after school."

Her heart swelled with pride. Fighting tears, she reached over to squeeze his shoulders. "Thank you, sweetheart. I know I can count on you." Then she ruffled his fair hair. "*You* concentrate on getting your math grade pulled up. Everything else will work out...you'll see."

But the smile fell from her face when she closed his door behind her. Even Jarrod sensed their financial situation was dire.

She peeked in on Maggie and Max and found both of them asleep on Maggie's bed, the thrill of sleeping with Mommy already forgotten.

She closed the bedroom door and looked in the direction of the garage, wondering if Octavia was still there. God forgive her—she hoped not. She wouldn't be surprised if Richard had covertly swung by to pick up Octavia and they were already back in Louisville. In fact, by the time Linda reached the garage, she was convinced her sister was long gone, returned to her perfect little world.

Linda opened the door and at the sight of Octavia reclining in the passenger seat of the minivan, her high heeled feet propped on the dashboard, her heart sank. She simply couldn't handle anything else right now.

She walked over to the window and rapped on it. Octavia started, then took her sweet time to buzz down the window, releasing a cloud of thin, white cigarette smoke. Classic rock crackled from the stereo speakers. The smell of beer permeated the interior of the van—and Octavia. She'd obviously found Sullivan's mini-fridge in the corner.

Linda coughed and waved her arms. "What are you doing, besides running down my battery?"

"Smoking," Octavia said with a loose smile, holding up a long cigarette with two limp fingers. She was drunk, and her words were runny. "I quit two years ago, but I always keep a pack with me, for emergencies. I figure this qualifies."

"Did you hear from Richard?"

"Nope."

"Did you call him?"

Octavia took a long drag, then exhaled on a smile. "Eighty-three times. No answer, and his voice mailbox is full. Apparently, I filled it."

"Oh. Do you have any idea where Richard might be?"

"Nope."

"I'm sure everything will look better in the morning—when you're sober. Why don't you come inside?"

"Is everybody gone?"

"Yes. The children and I are getting ready to go to bed. You can sleep here tonight."

Octavia took another drag and exhaled. "Where? This place is so junked up, I don't know how anyone can live here."

Linda flinched. She'd never been invited to Octavia's home in Louisville, but she was sure it was magnificent. "We manage."

"Besides," Octavia said with a flick of ashes, "you don't want me here."

Linda was caught off guard, and hesitated too long.

"Loud and clear," Octavia said, snubbing out her cigarette on the top of a beer can. "I'll go to a hotel."

"Wait—Octavia, of course I want you here...you're family."

Her sister gave a dry laugh. "Family? That's the lowest insult of all."

"Not for me," Linda said in a choked voice. "I've lost too much family."

Octavia scoffed. "You're lucky your husband died, Linda. It's the lesser of two evils."

The cruel remark took Linda's breath away, but she was too exhausted to react. "I'm going to bed now," she said through gritted teeth. "You're welcome to stay, Octavia. Or not."

She'd reached the door leading into the house when she heard the door to the van open and Octavia emerge with a clatter of empty beer cans falling on the concrete floor.

"Okay," Octavia slurred, "but just for tonight...to make sure you're okay." She wobbled on her high heels for a few steps, then stumbled and fell to her hands and knees.

Linda closed her eyes briefly, then walked back to help Octavia to her feet. Why couldn't she hate her sister? "You're bleeding," Linda chided, wiping at Octavia's knees.

"Funny...I don't feel anything."

Linda looked into her sister's vacant blue eyes and realized for once in their lives, they were occupying the same space on the emotional scale. "Let's get you inside and cleaned up."

Octavia allowed Linda to lead her to the master bathroom. Linda turned on the water and looked longingly at the shower, but pushed Octavia in the direction of the spray, then backtracked to Jarrod's room. He was burrowed under the covers, but roused long enough to endure a goodnight kiss.

"I know it feels like a tornado has torn through our lives," she whispered. "But tomorrow we'll start putting the pieces back together."

Jarrod just nodded and rolled over. He obviously wanted to close his eyes and put this horrible day behind him—she knew how he felt.

She checked on Maggie. Neither the little cherub nor Max stirred as Linda removed Maggie's shoes. Linda pressed a kiss to her fragrant curls, then retreated to the hallway and headed back to her bedroom. She toed off her low-heeled pumps and acknowledged a full-body ache she suspected might never leave. From the bathroom, the shower was still going.

Linda knocked on the bathroom door, and when she didn't get an answer, cracked it open. A trail of designer shoes and a balled up black dress led to Octavia sitting against the wall in her black underwear, snoring, oblivious to the running shower steaming up the room. Her stunning pieces of formal jewelry were incongruous next to her near nudity—a thick rope of gold fell past her collarbone, a chunky onyx and diamond bracelet, and several rings on both hands. Her scraped knees were raw and red, her face was blurry, and she stank of cheap beer and cigarettes. Octavia had maintained her lean-limbed cheerleader body, but at the moment she looked decidedly less than pert.

Linda stepped over her to turn off the shower. Octavia roused with a little snort. "Where am I?"

"In my junked up house," Linda said, leaning down to help her to her feet. "Come on, to bed with you." She stopped in her bedroom long enough to force a T-shirt over Octavia's head, then led her to the futon in the den, the unofficial "guest room." Octavia slumped in a chair while Linda wrestled to unfold the narrow, lumpy mattress. She retrieved a pillow and a sheet from a closet, and before she could tuck in the edges, Octavia had climbed onto the horizontal surface and collapsed.

Linda stared at her alien sister's sleeping figure, both comforted by and resentful of her presence. Octavia had a way of cutting people both ways. Hopefully, the impromptu visit would be of short duration.

She made her way back through the shambolic house that was deathly quiet and dark in the corners, reeking of potato salad and carnations.

It had been the most bizarrely horrific day of her life...and she had somehow lived through it.

That had to count for something.

When she crossed the threshold of her and Sullivan's bedroom, she stopped and stared at the big empty bed, still clad in the sheets he'd slept on mere days ago. Her throat closed as dread washed over her. But sleeping alone was only one of many aspects of her new reality, and the sooner she accepted it, the better. She switched off the overhead light, but quickly changed her mind and turned it back on.

Then Linda crawled into bed fully dressed, and pulled the covers over her head.

CHAPTER SEVEN

OCTAVIA JERKED AWAKE and instantly tensed. Something was very wrong. Was that...a baying dog?

She shifted, and a headache hit her like an ax to the frontal lobe. She gasped, then tried to blink the room into focus. She shifted her weight gingerly and pain knifed through her lower back. What on earth was this dilapidated piece of furniture she was lying on?

Fuzzy daylight streaming through windows indicated it was morning. The events of the previous day came flooding back to her. *Linda's house...Sullivan's funeral...Richard leaving her...their money gone.* Good God—it hadn't been a bad dream after all.

Her eyes welled with angry tears and she rolled to bury her face back into the pillow.

And stopped.

A small pink stuffed bear sat looking at her with big button eyes and an embroidered smile.

What the hell?

The baying had stopped, but slowly she registered sounds coming from the kitchen and little people voices—namely, the unmistakable voice of that sassy little Maggie.

Did the pint-sized princess ever shut up?

Desperate for aspirin and caffeine, Octavia pushed herself upright, snatched the stuffed animal and made her way toward the kitchen, stubbing her toe twice in the process. Every room was lined wall to wall with furniture and building supplies—the place was a tetanus shot waiting to happen.

She walked into the kitchen and blinked against the harsh overhead light. Damn, the injection sites in her face were sore. Jarrod and Maggie were sitting at the table, eating from mismatched plates. Their jowly dog stood with its paws on the window sill, staring out.

"What's his problem?" Octavia snapped.

"A squirrel keeps stealing the birdseed," Jarrod said.

"Wow, crime is rampant around here," Octavia said dryly. She found a drinking glass rather quickly since the cabinets didn't have doors on them. The cold water faucet was more tricky—there was some kind of tool attached to it.

"You have to turn the wrench," Jarrod supplied.

She pulled the tool toward her and filled her glass. "Where does your mother keep the aspirin?"

"In the cabinet over the refrigerator."

She rummaged through bottles of cough syrup and chewable vitamins until she found the aspirin, shook out a few into her hand, then tossed them back. She emptied the water glass with a long gulp, then turned around to find the kids staring at her.

"What?" she demanded.

"You look funny," Jarrod said.

Maggie wrinkled her pug nose. "And you smell yucky."

"Too bad," Octavia said, then held up the pink bear. "I guess this is yours?"

Maggie nodded exuberantly. "I thought you might want a friend."

Dammit, she was a sly little chubby thing. Octavia narrowed her eyes. "I have plenty of friends, thanks. Where's your mother?"

"We're letting her sleep in," Jarrod said. "We got ourselves ready for school."

"Interesting outfit," she said to Maggie, who looked like an acid trip.

Maggie dimpled. "Thank you."

"I don't guess you made coffee?" Octavia asked.

They shook their heads no.

"There's the coffeemaker," Jarrod said, pointing to a dated contraption sitting on the counter.

Fine, except she didn't feel like figuring out how to work it. Her stomach growled. She walked over to the table and eyed the greenish patties on their plates. "What are you eating?"

"Veggie sausage," Jarrod said with a frown. "Want some?"

"You can have mine," Maggie offered.

"No, thanks. Don't you have any cereal or something?"

"We're only allowed to eat it on special 'casions."

Octavia angled her head. "I declare today a special occasion."

"There's Captain Crunch on the top shelf behind the oatmeal," Jarrod said, setting his plate on the floor for the dog. "I'll get the bowls!"

She reached high and moved four—no, five—enormous canisters of oatmeal. "What's with all the oatmeal?"

"Mom won a bunch of it in a contest," Jarrod said. "She's always winning something."

"But nothing that tastes good," Maggie groused. "I'll get the milk." She set her plate on the floor next to Jarrod's where the dog was already digging in.

Jarrod set large mixing bowls on the table. Octavia filled them with cereal, and Maggie went behind her, pouring too much milk. The three of them sat down and dug in with giant spoons. Javier, her personal trainer, would have a heart attack if he saw the sugary meal, but right now, she needed an indulgence.

A heavy, warm weight fell on her feet. Octavia jumped, then looked under the table to see the wrinkly reddish brown dog laying across her feet.

"It means he likes you," Jarrod said with a laugh.

"I'm not a pet person," Octavia said.

"Max is more than a pet—he's a retired police bloodhound. He has medals and stuff."

"Yeah, well, right now he's just another male stepping on my toes," she muttered.

"This is better than veggie sausage," Maggie said with milk running down her chin. "You can make breakfast every morning, Aunt Tavey."

"Oh, no." Octavia wagged her spoon. "I'm not staying. I have my own home."

"Where?"

"Louisville."

54

"Where's that?"

"About an hour's drive in that direction." She waved vaguely in the air.

"Louisville Cardinals," Jarrod added with a boo and a hiss.

Octavia nodded to his shirt. "You're a UK fan, I see."

He puffed up. "Yeah. I'm gonna play basketball for them someday."

"I was a UK cheerleader."

His eyes widened. "No kidding? Cool."

"Where are your pom poms?" Maggie asked suspiciously.

"At my home," Octavia returned.

"Can I have them?"

"You're not supposed to ask for things," Jarrod chided.

"It's okay," Octavia said. "If you don't ask, you never know. But no, you can't have my pom poms. They're *mine*."

Maggie seemed unfazed. "Did you lose your husband?"

Touché. "No. He just...went on vacation."

"Without you?" Jarrod asked.

She frowned. "Don't you two have to finish getting ready for school?"

"Can you fix our lunches?" Maggie asked.

Octavia wiped the milk from her mouth with her hand. "That depends—what do you want?"

"Marshmallows!"

"I can do that." She looked at Jarrod. "How about you?"

He grinned. "Oreos."

"Coming right up." She dislodged Max and pushed to her feet, retrieved two paper bags from the stack on the counter, then stuffed them full with the treats she found on the top shelf. This parenting thing wasn't so hard.

Jarrod looked out the window. "Here comes Mrs. Boyd, Maggie. Get your backpack."

The kids scrambled, then ran for the front door, grabbing their lunch bags on the way. Octavia followed them to the door, then walked out on the stoop, conceding she probably should know who her niece and nephew left with. A heavy, stiff-looking woman she recognized as one of the people she'd herded out of Linda's house gaped up at her, then marched closer.

"Don't you think you're dressed rather inappropriately to be outside?"

Octavia looked down at the unfamiliar T-shirt sporting a smiley face and realized her La Perla underwear was on display. "Nice to see you, too, um—?"

"Nan Boyd. I escort the neighborhood kids to the bus stop. But I must say, I think it's too soon for Jarrod and Maggie to go back to school after what they've been through."

"Well," Octavia said sweetly, "thank goodness it's none of your ding dang business." She waved to the kidlets, then went back into the house and slammed the door.

Now officially in a sour mood, she picked up the cordless phone and dialed Richard's cell phone, thinking if he didn't recognize the number, he might answer.

He didn't.

So she called their house.

"Habersham residence," their maid Carla said.

Octavia frowned—she wasn't as certain as Richard that Carla hadn't stolen her watch. "Carla, it's Mrs. Habersham. Is my husband there, by chance?"

"Mr. Habersham? I thought he was with you in Lexington, ma'am."

"He...um, was. But a business matter came up and he had to leave. I thought I might catch him at home."

"No, ma'am. I haven't seen him. And the master bed wasn't slept in last night."

Octavia's stomach tightened. "Oh...well, he must have pulled an all-nighter at the office, or been called out of town. When you see him, will you please ask him to call me on my cell phone?"

"Of course, ma'am. Um...ma'am, when I got here this morning, there was a letter taped to the front door."

Octavia's pulse picked up—had Richard left a note? "What kind of letter?"

"The envelope says it's from the Jefferson County Sheriff's Office."

She exhaled. "It's probably about one of Mr. Habersham's cases. Just leave it on his desk."

"Yes, ma'am. Oh, and one more thing. The check you gave me this week... the bank wouldn't cash it."

Octavia swallowed a curse and forced false cheer into her voice. "Mr. Habersham moved some of our bank accounts and forgot to tell me. He or I will pay you as soon as we see you."

"Yes, ma'am."

She disconnected the call and backtracked to the van in search of her purse while her heart trotted in her chest. She checked her wallet for cash—a little over six hundred dollars. That wouldn't last long. She forced herself to tamp down the panic as she called to check account balances and the available limit on her credit cards.

"Cancelled?"

"On hold?"

"Deactivated?"

"Closed?"

"Stopped?"

"Blocked?"

At the end of the stack, she had a Macy's Department Store card that was still active, and a gas card. An old savings account contained nine hundred dollars. Every other account was overdrawn or cancelled.

She had her jewelry case with her, but no way was she going to sell her good pieces.

Octavia brought her fist to her mouth. She had to get back to Louisville and figure out what was going on.

A noise sounded from the hallway. She looked up to see Linda skid to a halt, still wearing yesterday's funeral dress, her eyes wide. "I overslept. Where are the kids?"

"Fed and on their way to the bus stop with your fat neighbor."

"What about their lunches?"

"Don't worry—I fixed them."

Linda heaved a sigh. "Thank you. I need coffee." She moved toward the coffeemaker and hit a series of buttons. "How did you sleep?"

"That thing I woke up on is a torture device."

"Sorry. Sullivan and I—" Linda stopped and blanched. "We don't have many guests."

Octavia's heart shifted. Damn Sullivan Smith for leaving her sister in a lurch. Damn men everywhere, dammit. "Did you get some rest?"

"Some," Linda said in an unconvincing voice. "Do I look as bad as you do?"

"Worse."

"At least I don't smell as bad as you do. Milk or sugar?"

"Do you have half and half?"

"I have milk and I have sugar. Wait—" She held up the empty jug. "We're out of milk."

"I'll have it black."

Linda brought two mugs to the table and they sat in silence. There was too much to talk about, none of it pleasant. The clutter of the demolitioned kitchen seem to close in on them. Octavia felt claustrophobic and antsy, her mind swirling. Some of her conversation with Linda the previous night was starting to come back to her. She'd been drunk, but it was no excuse for some of the things she'd said—no matter how true. And she felt bad for Linda, but she didn't want to get involved in her sister's life. She had her own problems to deal with.

Linda sipped. "Have you heard from Richard?"

Octavia sipped. "No."

Linda sipped. "And you still don't know why he left?"

Octavia sipped. "No." Although she wondered now about the phone call he'd taken yesterday on the drive here that had upset him...and later when she'd seen him sitting in the car talking on the phone, gesturing in anger. Obviously their financial problems had reached a boiling point.

She could feel her sister's censure wafting in her direction. And the longer the silence dragged on, the more it rankled Octavia. Who was Linda to judge? "Go ahead...say it."

Linda blinked. "Say what?"

"This is what I get for marrying Richard for his money."

"I would never say that. Besides, I don't know enough about your and Richard's relationship to have an opinion."

"That's right, you don't," Octavia snapped. She took another sip to cover the fact that her eyes had filled with unwanted tears. After a few blinks, though, she couldn't fight the panic anymore and a sob escaped her.

Linda reached across the table to clasp her hand. "It's going to be okay."

But the dam had burst, sweeping away Octavia's pride and revealing her low-lying vulnerabilities. The seed of doubt in her mind when she'd walked down the aisle all those years ago had grown over the years, but she'd ignored it...and now she had a solid mass weighing down her heart. "Don't you see, Linda? It's *not* going to be okay. I did everything wrong. I chose a lavish life with Richard over having a family or a career of my own. If we're broke, I'll have nothing to show for it. And I'm going to be the laughingstock of all my friends."

Linda's silence rang in the air like a cry of victory. She had children, and the dignity of being a widow, while Octavia was simply discarded alongside the road like a sack of garbage.

Her sister got up and came back with a box of tissue. "So what now?"

Octavia blew her nose noisily. "Will you take me home? I need to find Richard."

Linda walked to the window. Octavia knew Linda was going to tell her she had too much on her own plate to be pulled into Octavia's problems, that she had a thousand errands today to run herself. And after being so insensitive to Linda's situation, she deserved to be snubbed. She was a terrible sister, and she wouldn't blame Linda if she told her to rent a car or call a cab, neither of which she could afford.

Linda heaved a sigh and turned back. "Well, you can't stay in this junked up place. Can you be ready in thirty minutes?"

CHAPTER EIGHT

"DID WE HAVE to bring the dog?"

Linda turned an amused smile toward Octavia in the passenger seat. Max stood on the back floorboard with his paws on the console and his head jutted between the two front seats, tongue lolling. "Max isn't bothering anyone."

At the sound of his name, he woofed.

"Speak for yourself. He's getting slobber all over the sleeve of my blouse."

"That would be the sleeve of *my* blouse," Linda corrected. She took perverse satisfaction in the fact that Octavia had to borrow some of her discount clothes to wear.

"And on that subject, let me just say that capri pants are the single worst fashion fraud ever perpetrated on American women," Octavia chirped.

"You look fine," Linda said with a laugh. "No one can see the labels on the inside."

"A discerning person doesn't have to see labels."

"You know the saying 'beggars can't be choosers'?"

Octavia sniffed. "I'm calling my accountant."

Linda shook her head—Octavia was a master at deflecting conversation when it suited her.

It was another beautiful spring morning in the Bluegrass, with plenty of turquoise sky and white clouds. Trees were fuzzy with new leaves and bulb flowers nodded along Versailles Road. There were faster routes to Louisville, but none so pretty, with its stacked limestone walls bordering the road and white board fences that delineated the sprawling horse farms the area was famous for.

Unbidden tears filled her eyes. Sullivan would never again see the beauty of a perfect spring day. Why hadn't they gone on more picnics? Taken the kids hiking?

Because they'd assumed they had tomorrow.

Octavia's shrill voice broke into her thoughts. "So help me, Frank, if you know where Richard is and you're not telling me, I'll put your balls in a sling-shot....There *has* to be some money somewhere....Then what am I supposed to live on?...Are you insane? I'm *not* going to sell my jewelry....Fax a report of where we stand financially to the house, I'm on my way there....Yeah, well you have a nice fucking day, too, Frank." Octavia stabbed the End button. "When is someone going to come up with an app that makes it sound like you hung up on the other person?"

Linda cringed. "I'm not sure you should be alienating your accountant right now."

Octavia whipped out a mirror and pressed a finger to the crease between her eyebrows. She looked pained. "For all I know, he could be taking advantage of Richard's absence...maybe he took our money and is lying about everything."

Linda didn't offer her opinion. Guilt gnawed at her for mourning the bounced ten thousand dollar check Octavia had given her. Yes, she was eager to deposit Octavia back into her own world (and out of theirs), but another reason she'd offered to drive her sister home was to escape...escape the bill collectors calling and the overdue notices stuffed in her mailbox. Today was Friday...she'd give herself until Monday before she hit the panic button.

For now, God help her, it made her feel a tad better to know that even wealthy people could have financial problems.

She turned to look at Octavia, but Octavia was staring out the window. In the distance, a sleek thoroughbred galloped through a lush field with her foal running along beside her, all legs and head. Her sister always had a soft spot for horses, had taken riding lessons when she was young, and begged their father to buy her a pony to train.

Nelson Guy's parenting style could best be described as "uneven." Sometimes he would leave the girls to their own devices to the point of neglect, and other times he would appear and shower them with expensive, impractical gifts. During his long absences they were forced to pool their babysitting money for groceries, then Nelson would return with Italian leather jackets for both of them or a giant TV for the living room, and once—a pony for Octavia.

Of course, Nelson rarely thought past lunch, so little details like where the horse would be stabled and fed, had escaped him. The pony had subsequently been taken away. Octavia had been despondent.

"Have you talked to our old man lately?" Octavia asked.

Apparently, they'd been remembering the same story. "I called him last month on his birthday. We talked for a while."

"What on earth about?"

"The kids mostly...but he always asks about you."

"Please don't tell him anything about my life."

"It's not as if I know a lot of details to share," Linda pointed out. "I usually just tell him that you're well."

"For how much longer will he be locked up?"

"Eight months, I think."

"Good God, what a wasted life. The Guy family legacy."

Words of protest sprang to Linda's tongue, but she couldn't in good conscience argue, not when she was questioning her own choices. They rode in silence for a few minutes, each of them marinating in their own melancholy. At least when they were young, they were optimistic their adult lives would be better than their childhood. Now...

"What are you going to do?" Octavia asked.

"About what?"

"About everything. How will you and the kids survive? Did Sullivan have life insurance?"

"We'll manage," Linda said evasively. "The children will receive social security until they're out of high school."

"That can't be much."

"I'll get a job."

"Doing what?"

Linda frowned. "I have skills."

"Did you ever finish your degree?"

She'd always intended to. "No."

"Jarrod said something this morning about you winning prizes?"

"Oh. I enter contests, just for fun, and sometimes I win little things."

"Like a pallet of Kleenex?"

"Yes." She sighed, thinking of how many boxes she'd already depleted.

"You could've been anything you wanted to be," Octavia said, her voice full of disapproval.

Linda bristled. "I am what I want to be—I'm a mother, and wife—" She broke off, remembering with a start that she was no longer a wife. She wiped her hand over her mouth, determined to keep the tears at bay. "My children keep me busy."

"Being busy is not the same as being fulfilled."

"Oh? And are you fulfilled, Octavia?"

Octavia's mouth tightened. "I'm...recognized."

"As Richard Habersham's wife," Linda added quietly. "*You* could've been anything you wanted to be."

"Who says I'm not?"

"Your entire body says so."

Octavia turned to stare at the passing landscape. Linda bit down on the inside of her cheek, regretting her remarks. But her sister's comments had landed too close to their mark—a few days ago she'd been lamenting that she wasn't feeling fulfilled...and look where it had gotten her.

God, what a mess. She gripped the steering wheel. If not for Jarrod and Maggie, she'd be tempted to drop off Octavia, and keep driving until the van ran out of gas...and just start over.

As if he sensed the tension in the vehicle, Max woofed to break the silence, then began to bay.

"What's his problem?" Octavia asked, putting her fingers in her ears.

"He probably needs to be walked," she said, reaching out to quiet Max with a pat. "How much further?"

"About twenty miles or so."

They were entering the outskirts of Louisville, a rambling river city steeped in history and tradition, much like Lexington. Louisville was world renowned for the Kentucky Derby and as the hub of the horse industry, but insiders knew the heart of the business was in Lexington and Versailles, where limestone-fed bluegrass made for strong equine bones, and the yearling sales drew international buyers.

Linda had always perceived Louisville to be the older sister to Lexington... and a bit of a bully.

Not unlike the Guy family dynamic.

"He's kind of an old dog for the kids, don't you think?" Octavia observed with a frown.

"Max is a retired police bloodhound. He helped solve lots of missing persons cases. Bloodhounds' sense of smell is so sensitive, they can distinguish human skin cells that are shed and passed out of a car's exhaust."

Octavia seemed unimpressed, fanning her hand in the air. "You'd think he could smell his own bad breath."

Linda laughed. "Max is too old to track long distances now, but he's a good watch dog, very protective of the kids."

"Protective is good," her sister murmured almost absent-mindedly.

Linda suspected she was thinking they could've used some protection when they were children. After their mother had left, they'd really only had each other, and Octavia had borne the brunt of the responsibility for herself and her younger sister. Linda's heart softened...no wonder her sister was so tough—she'd always had to be.

"Turn here," Octavia said, gesturing.

As they entered an upscale residential area, her sister became more antsy, fidgeting and sitting on the edge of her seat. Her head pivoted, and Linda realized she was looking for Richard or his car. With every turn they made, the houses got bigger and more impressive. At length, they turned into a gatehouse. When they stopped, a guard came out and Linda buzzed down the window.

"It's me—Mrs. Habersham," Octavia said, waving from the passenger seat.

The guard nodded in recognition, but his face looked tense. "Welcome home, ma'am." He glanced at the aged minivan with skepticism and looked as if he were about to add something else, then he opened a gate and waved them through.

"What do you drive?" Linda asked as she wove her way through the afflu-ent neighborhood, following Octavia's directions.

"A Jag convertible."

Of course she did, Linda thought with a stab of envy. Money didn't buy happiness, but it could certainly lubricate the sad times.

"It's the gray house on the right," Octavia said, pointing.

And what a house it was. Linda pulled into the driveway slowly and gaped. It was a compound, the brick mansion and grounds easily as large as a com-mercial building, and perfectly manicured. She pulled up and parked in front of the four-car garage.

"Wow," was all she could say.

"Okay, well, thanks for the ride," Octavia said, leaning forward for a quick hug.

So she wasn't even going to invite her inside. That stung, but Linda herself had been eager to deliver Octavia back to her world so she could return to her own.

"You're welcome," Linda said. "Do you mind if I walk Max before I leave?"

Octavia hesitated. "Okay...just keep him out of the flowers."

"Don't worry," Linda said, holding up a plastic bag. "I'll clean up after him."

Octavia wrinkled her nose. "Goodbye, Linda....call me sometime."

Sometime—not when or if she needed her, but sometime. And it was clear Octavia didn't intend to call her.

"Sure," Linda said.

Octavia climbed out of the van and marched toward the front door of the colossal house, then walked inside without looking back.

"Come on, Max," Linda said, waving him out of the van. She looked back to the closed front door, fighting unexpected tears. "Do your business so we can get out of here."

CHAPTER NINE

OCTAVIA CLOSED THE door behind her, and puffed her cheeks out in an exhale. She knew it was rude not to ask Linda to come inside, but she wanted to be alone to sort things out...and to confront Richard if he was home.

"Richard?"

Her voice echoed in the soaring two-story entryway. Gleaming black marble flooring was the perfect foil for the sweeping white double staircase that led to the respective wings of the house. A dazzling three-tiered chandelier that hung over the shared landing winked a welcome. She inhaled the scent of freesia that she'd selected as her signature home fragrance and savored the silence for a few seconds—no boisterous neighbors, kids, or dogs.

But no husband either?

"Richard?" she shouted in a decibel that would pierce even his closed office door on the second floor.

No answer.

If the coward were there, his Mercedes would be in the garage. She marched through the vast dining room with the table that seated twenty-two, the massive kitchen with commercial grade appliances, and the mud room (which had never seen a speck of mud), to the door leading to the garage and flung it open.

It took a few seconds for her to register the fact that Richard's car was not in its usual parking spot...and neither was her Jag convertible.

Nor the backup BMW.

Panic nipped at her. What was going on?

She heard a noise behind her and turned to see Carla standing there in her gray uniform dress, with a fearful look on her pretty face. "Mrs. Habersham—"

She stopped and looked Octavia up and down, clearly surprised by the way she was dressed.

Octavia gritted her teeth. "*What*, Carla?"

"Some men came...they had these papers to take the cars." She held up a handful of neon-colored forms. "I couldn't stop them."

Her head swam. "Has my husband called?"

"No." But Carla wasn't making eye contact.

"What aren't you telling me?"

Carla looked up. "Some things are gone."

"What kinds of things?"

"The silver."

"The silver?"

"And the framed drawing in the library."

"The Picasso?"

"And some of Mr. Habersham's clothing."

Swallowing hard, Octavia pushed past Carla and hurried upstairs to their bedroom. She threw open the door to Richard's walk-in closet and noted that more clothes were missing than were required for a weekend in Lexington. A check of his jewelry case confirmed her worst suspicions: His most cherished watches and cufflinks were gone. It seemed he'd planned an extended trip—without her.

She raced to Richard's office. His laptop was gone, no surprise. She opened drawers in his desk to find them virtually empty—where were their personal financial records? On the fax machine was the summary report Frank had promised to send. Every line item sent her heart sliding lower. Not only were their accounts empty, but their debt was gut-clenching, their mortgage payments—and everything else—months overdue.

How could Richard have kept this from her?

She glanced around the room blindly, and in the back of her mind, registered something was out of place. She scanned the room again and her gaze settled on the bookshelf behind Richard's desk. Not out of place—something was gone: the twenty thousand dollar Chihuly glass bowl she'd given him for his birthday.

She leaned into his massive mahogany desk to keep from falling down... and spotted the letter Carla had described from the sheriff's office, the one that had been taped to the front door.

Octavia picked up the envelope, ran her finger under the flap, and pulled out the folded sheet of paper. *Writ of Eviction*. They had fourteen days to remove their personal belongings from the foreclosed property.

Foreclosed.

It wasn't possible. Not her big, gorgeous home, her trophy of success. The words on the page blurred. There were ways to stop foreclosure...weren't there? She'd only half-listened to the news as the foreclosure epidemic had rolled over the country—it hadn't pertained to her.

She picked up the cordless phone from Richard's desk and hit the speed dial button for his direct line at his office. The phone rang two, three times, then Richard's voice came over the line.

A recording. "This is Richard Habersham. I've stepped away from my desk—"

She cursed and threw the phone across the room. It hit a wall and exploded before crashing to the floor.

On the eviction notice she wrote with a black felt-tip marker "Fix this, Frank!!!!" and faxed it to the accountant's office. She stood still for several minutes and tried to breathe, tried to calm her sprinting heart. Bright spots flashed behind her eyes. This could not be happening.

The fax machine kicked on and she saw a response was coming from Frank's office. She heaved a sigh of relief—Frank would know what to do. She waited as the hand-written message scrolled out of the machine.

I can't make any promises. And there is the matter of my outstanding bill. Have you been able to reach Richard?

She crunched the piece of paper in her hands.

The rumble of a loud vehicle arriving outside brought her head around. She hurried to the window and looked down on the front yard. A large delivery truck from a local big box electronics store had backed up in the driveway. Surely Richard hadn't ordered yet another piece of equipment for his prized home theater.

How would they pay for it?

The doorbell sounded like a gong in the house. A few seconds later, Carla's panicked voice rang out. "Mrs. Habersham!"

What now? Octavia thought as she moved to the top of the stairs.

Two meaty looking men were walking through the entryway, heading toward the rear of the house where the home theater was located. "We're here to repossess the flat screen, and the sound system," one of them said without breaking stride.

Oh, dear God—carry out the equipment while her neighbors gawked? Tongues were probably already wagging from their vehicles being towed away. And weren't foreclosures announced in the newspaper?

"No!" she shouted, and jogged down the stairs, made more problematic by the cheap flip-flops of Linda's she wore. By the time she flapped to the bottom, the men were coming back through the foyer, with speakers under their arms.

"You can't do this," she yelled, following them outside. "Put those back!" She tugged on one of their shirts ineffectively.

"Step back, lady," one of the guys threatened.

From out of nowhere came the sound of a growling dog. Octavia whirled to see Max straining in an aggressive stance toward the men, his teeth bared, his leash dragging behind him. He barked and snarled as if he might tear off a limb.

"Call off your dog, lady," one of the men shouted. "We're just doing our job."

Octavia's estimation of the big wrinkly hound rose a few notches, but he'd also caused a big, fat scene. Neighbors had emerged to see what the commotion was all about. Across the street, Emily Devonshire waved, then cupped her hands to call, "Is everything alright?"

Octavia waved back. "Oh, yes! We're just replacing our old TV. Thanks, though!" Nosy witch. Octavia turned back to the men and muttered, "Hurry the hell up."

Linda came bounding up and retrieved the end of Max's leash. "Sorry, sis, he got away from me." She quieted the dog with a stern command, then murmured, "What's going on?"

"None of your business," Octavia snapped, stinging with humiliation. "Why are you still here?"

Linda blanched. "Sorry for the trouble. We're going now."

Octavia instantly regretted her outburst, then reminded herself she didn't have time for regrets, not when her life was imploding right in front of her. She couldn't find Richard. She was broke. She had no transportation. And in two weeks, she'd have no place to live. She considered her options, which amounted to one, then swore under her breath. "Linda...wait."

Her sister turned back.

"I'm sorry I lost my temper." Octavia wet her lips. "I need a place to stay for a little while, until things settle down."

Linda gave a laugh. "Are you kidding me?"

Octavia wondered if she'd finally pushed her sister too far...and for a split second, she almost wished Linda would show some spunk, even if it was at her expense.

Linda pulled her hand over her mouth. "You're welcome to stay with us, but you know what the accommodations are like."

"I can handle adversity," Octavia said charitably.

Linda looked heavenward, then said, "Do you want to follow me home?"

"Actually...I'll need to ride with you."

"Why?"

"My car isn't available."

"O...kay. I assume you'll want to pack a suitcase?"

"Give me a few minutes to grab some essentials." She dodged the men coming out carrying the massive flat screen TV that Richard had been so ecstatic over when it had been delivered, and suddenly, she was glad to see it go.

"Carla!" she shouted as she walked into the house.

The woman appeared, looking teary. "Yes, Mrs. Habersham?"

"I need your help to gather some personal things."

"You're leaving?" The woman looked apprehensive.

She didn't want to ignite more gossip...nor did she want Carla to find a new position in case she and Richard were able to set things right with the mortgage. "I'm going to stay with my sister for a while. She just lost her husband, you know."

Octavia hurried to her bedroom and threw open her own enormous walk-in closet and instructed Carla to put her suitcases on the bed.

"All of them?"

"Er...I don't know exactly what I'll need while I'm there," Octavia hedged. She grabbed armfuls of clothes and dumped them into the open cases, hangers and all. When they ran out of suitcases and trunks, Carla fetched a stack of heavy duty garbage bags to hold shoes and handbags. Octavia longed to change clothes, but she didn't dare stop long enough. Instead she tied a Hermes scarf around her neck to spice up her lame outfit.

When they were finished bagging everything, Octavia looked up and felt a surge of affection for Carla...the woman deserved to know the truth.

"To be honest, Carla, I don't know when Mr. Habersham or I will be back, so you should try to find another position if you can."

The woman looked crestfallen, but she nodded. "Do you think Mr. Habersham is safe?"

Until I find him. Then Octavia squinted. "Why would you think he wouldn't be?"

Carla looked over her shoulder, as if she were afraid someone else was listening. "Two days ago Mr. Habersham gave me something to keep for him."

Octavia frowned. "What did he give you?"

Carla hesitated, then reached into her pocket and withdrew a small padded envelope.

"What is it?" Octavia took the package.

"He didn't say and I didn't ask."

A stamp of Richard's legal insignia spanned the sealed edge of the envelope. The date two days prior and Richard's initials were scribbled on the insignia in his handwriting. Otherwise, there were no markings on it. A small heavy object had settled into the corner, but it was impossible to identify the item. A ring? A coin?

"When did Richard say he'd be back to get it?"

"He didn't say," Carla murmured. "But I've kept it with me. And now you say you and Mr. Habersham might not be back...I didn't want to disappear with it."

"You did the right thing by giving it to me." But inside she fumed. What was Richard thinking giving Carla something valuable for safekeeping? He knew she suspected the woman of taking her diamond watch.

Then a horrible thought occurred to her. She marched to her jewelry hutch and threw open the doors.

Carla gasped. "Where's all your jewelry?"

Octavia's eyes narrowed. "I was about to ask you the same thing." She had her exclusive jewels with her, but even her second-tier jewelry was pretty darn valuable.

The woman's eyes widened and she began to back up. "I—I didn't take anything, Mrs. Habersham. I swear, I would never do that."

Octavia believed her—dammit. Because she had a feeling Richard had cleaned out her jewelry box along with his own...and considering the state of their finances, he was probably the culprit behind her missing watch, too. It was like a kick in the teeth.

"Don't worry, Carla. I believe you." She rummaged through what was left of the jewelry and came up with a modest pair of diamond stud earrings—the kind one might wear grocery shopping—and put them in Carla's hand. "Thank you for your help and your service."

"I couldn't take these," Carla protested.

"You can and you will." Octavia tilted her jewelry hutch forward and emptied the loose baubles into an empty purse. "It's the least I can do for you carrying all these bags down to my sister's van. If you hurry, you can get them all loaded before that enormous truck leaves, so the neighbors won't see you."

Carla surveyed the mound of suitcases and bulging bags with a watery smile, but she nodded and tucked the earrings into a pocket.

Octavia dropped the mysterious padded envelope into the purse along with the jewelry to deal with later. On the way out of the house, she picked up the unopened mail lying on a foyer table and stuffed it inside, too—one of the envelopes might contain a check.

Tears pricked her eyelids as she drank in the details of the extravagant home she'd so painstakingly put together, candlestick by candlestick. She refused to cry—this wasn't the end...she simply wouldn't let it be.

But her hatred for Richard was growing by the moment. Leaving her was one thing, but leaving her exposed like this was simply unforgivable.

He. Would. Pay.

CHAPTER TEN

"SEE, I TOLD YOU it would all fit," Octavia said as Linda slid the van door closed.

"Barely." Linda bit her lip as she surveyed how low the loaded van sat on its worn out tires. "Have you seen my home? I don't know where we're going to put all this stuff."

"It's temporary," her sister assured her. "Now let's get out of here before that big-ass truck leaves." Octavia hopped into the passenger seat and slammed the door.

Linda looked down at Max, who looked up at her. "Come on." She led him around to Octavia's door and rapped on the window.

Octavia cracked open the door. "What?"

Linda gestured to the bags overflowing between the two front seats. "Max is going to have to sit on your lap."

"No way."

"Yes way, unless you want to drive."

Octavia frowned. "I refuse to drive a minivan."

Linda patted the seat next to Octavia. "Up, Max."

The dog obeyed and she settled him across her sister's lap under much protest. Linda smiled to herself as she circled back to climb into the driver's seat. She started the engine. "So what's going on? Are you leaving Richard?"

"No. I'm merely leaving my house." Octavia shifted under the weight of an unwieldy Max and made a face. "It seems we've been foreclosed on."

Linda's mouth dropped in shock. "Foreclosed?"

"My CPA will handle everything," Octavia said with a dismissive wave. "I'm sure it's a matter of crossed paperwork or something. Now let's get going."

Linda hoped she would be so calm when *her* house was foreclosed upon. "I don't guess you've talked to Richard?"

"That would be no."

Octavia had nothing more to add as they wove back through the neighborhood. After they exited the gate, she pointed in the direction opposite the Interstate. "Turn here."

"Where are we going?"

"To Richard's office."

"He's there?"

"He'd better hope not."

Linda studied her sister's determined profile and the thought crossed her mind that she didn't relish being in the middle of a confrontation. But she knew Octavia when she got something in her head, so she kept quiet and kept driving.

A few minutes later, Octavia directed her to pull into an office park.

From the size of the white one-story building that heralded "Habersham Law Office" in gilded letters on its front picture window, Richard appeared to be doing well for himself. The exterior of the building resembled a residence, with a small front porch and plant bed, ringed with perennials. Very homey.

Right down to the "Closed—Please Visit Again Soon" sign posted on the front door.

"Back in next to those trees," Octavia said, pointing to a spot across the parking lot.

Linda frowned, but did as she asked.

"I'll be right back," Octavia said. "How do I get the hound off of me?"

"I'll get him," Linda said. "He might need to be walked again." She alighted and walked around to open the passenger door. Then she helped Max down—his arthritic legs didn't let him bounce like he used to.

"I'll take him for a walk," Octavia offered. "Hook him up."

Linda lifted one eyebrow, especially when Octavia removed the scarf around her neck, wrapped it around her dark hair, and tied it under her chin.

With her big, designer sunglasses, her face was almost completely covered. But she hooked on Max's leash and handed it to Octavia, along with a plastic bag.

"What's this for?"

"In case he has to go."

"Are you insane?" Octavia shoved the bag back into Linda's hand. "I don't pick up dog shit." She shook the leash. "Come on, you."

Linda watched bemused as Octavia crossed the rather long parking lot, practically dragging Max behind her. She approached the office door with composure. She tried the doorknob, but it was obviously locked. She cupped her hands around her eyes and peered inside. Then, presumably disappointed, Octavia allowed Max to explore the flower bed.

Linda felt a stab of pity for her high-strung sister—she had to be frustrated beyond belief, yet she was handling her husband being missing better than Linda thought possible.

A group of teenage boys walked by. Octavia bent over and Linda wondered if her sister had had a change of heart about cleaning up after Max. Then, as quick as a snake striking, Octavia picked up a brick and hurled it through the big gilt-lettered window.

Immediately, an alarm sounded. Max began to howl. Octavia pointed a finger to the passing teens, shouting at them, as if one of them had done it. They looked bewildered. Octavia yanked Max away, pointing and shouting at the boys. Pedestrians stopped to stare. The teens scattered like ants.

Linda stared in stunned silence as Octavia strode back to the van and climbed inside. It took some time for her and Max to get settled, then she turned her head toward Linda.

"What?"

"Are you out of your mind?" Linda sputtered. "You could be arrested!"

Octavia untied the scarf and scoffed. "Everyone thinks one of those kids did it."

"Well, I hope you feel better."

"I will if Richard shows up." She offered up a glib smile. "When the alarm goes off, he gets an automated call on his cell phone. If he's within driving distance, he'll show up. Nothing means more to Richard than his practice."

Linda pursed her mouth. Good thinking.

They were tucked far enough away from the spectacle that no one would notice them, but still Linda's heart pounded. Max lifted his head and bayed.

"Can't you shut him up?" Octavia snapped.

"The alarm probably hurts his ears," Linda said, but rubbed his head to quiet him.

A security officer arrived on the scene first, then a police car. The alarm continued to wail. The police talked to a bystander who waved in the direction the teenagers had gone. Notes were taken. Much head-scratching ensued. More gawkers arrived.

But no Richard.

At length, the alarm stopped. A repairman showed up with a toolbox and a piece of plywood to cover the broken window. Within forty-five minutes, everyone was gone.

Linda could tell that Octavia was bitterly disappointed.

"We can wait a few more minutes," she offered, although they'd be cutting it close to get home before the kids.

"No." Octavia sat back in the seat. "Let's go."

Linda started the van and pulled out. "Would any of his friends know where he is, or maybe his secretary?"

"I called them and no. His secretary said he told her he had a family emergency, and needed to close the office for a couple of weeks. His friends haven't heard from him."

"Have you contacted his family?"

"There's only his brother in Denver, and they're not close. I called him and he hasn't talked to Richard since the holidays."

She decided this wasn't the best time to point out that the two of *them* usually only spoke during the holidays. "Are you going to report him missing? I can ask Detective Hall to make some inquiries."

"I don't know what I'm going to do."

From the utter despair in her voice, Linda knew Octavia was referring to more than Richard. She glanced at her glamorous sister, who was accustomed to valet parking and personal shoppers, now reduced to wearing discount clothes and sharing her seat in a minivan with a dog, and her heart contracted.

"I have a confession to make," Linda said.

Octavia looked suspicious. "What?"

"This morning, when you said you'd done everything wrong..."

"You have to remind me?"

"No. I didn't say anything because...that's how I feel, too." Linda wet her lips. "I chose a family over a career, and I put all my energy into Sullivan and what he wanted out of life. And now...look at me." She blinked back tears. "I don't know what I'm going to do either."

Octavia gave a little laugh. "We're a fine pair. I wish I could help you financially, Linda, but I can't."

"And I wish—" Linda stopped. "Wait...maybe I can help you."

"You're giving me a place to stay."

"No, I mean I have Sullivan's agency."

"What about it?"

"Well, I'll have to shut it down, of course. But I know the agency has access to information that's not available to the average citizen. Maybe we can use those resources to find Richard."

Octavia sat up. "Really?"

Linda shrugged. "We can try. I have to go by the agency tomorrow to talk to the office manager about closing out the books and ending the lease."

"Okay...it's a start."

Linda's phone rang, and it was just out of reach. Her heart jumped to her throat—had one of the kids changed their mind about school and wanted to come home? "Can you see who's calling?"

Octavia picked it up and glanced at the screen. "Oakley Hall."

She hesitated, then shook her head. "Let it roll over to voice mail."

Octavia arched a brow. "He seems very...attentive."

Linda shifted in her seat. "He's Sullivan's best friend. He's just concerned."

"Oakley Hall...why is he familiar to me?"

"I, uh...might've dated him once."

"Only once?"

"Maybe twice."

"Do tell," Octavia said, leaning close. Even Max perked an ear.

"Nothing to tell," Linda said breezily. "I met Oakley first, but as it turned out, Sullivan and I were more suited."

"Hm."

"How long have you lived in your house?" Linda asked to change the subject.

As expected, Octavia's face lit up as she gushed about her home, and described each room in excruciating detail since Linda hadn't seen the inside. She pretended to be interested as they retraced their route back to Lexington, but her mind jumped ahead to the end of her little adventure that had allowed her to keep everything at bay for a few hours.

Her heart grew heavier and heavier as they neared her house. By the time they pulled into the garage, she was fighting tears again. She didn't want to be there without Sullivan. And the piles of dusty building materials were an acute reminder of just how many things were left undone.

She didn't want to go inside to the mess, to the stack of thank you notes she had to write and the messages of sympathy in the mailbox and on the phone.

Just as the panic started to overwhelm her, the kids arrived home from school. She passed out hugs and kisses and asked them about the party and the basketball game. They were talkative and seemed happy to see "Aunt Tavey." When she looked at them smiling, she could almost pretend nothing was wrong.

"Are you moving in, Aunt Tavey?" Maggie asked.

"No. I'm just staying for a few days."

"Good. Can I have marshmallows for lunch again tomorrow?"

"And Oreos?" Jarrod added.

Linda gave Octavia a questioning look, but her sister shook her head as if she had no idea what they were talking about.

"How about pizza for dinner?" Octavia asked.

The kids cheered, but Linda's mind raced to the money they shouldn't be spending.

"It's on me," Octavia offered.

A nice gesture, but she knew her sister's funds were dwindling, too. "Jarrod, show Aunt Tavey where we keep the pizza coupons."

While the three of them headed toward the kitchen, Linda thumbed through the mail and sighed at the number of sympathy cards—all well intended, but draining. A little envelope symbol on the phone indicated there were messages waiting. She dialed into voice mail and listened with a closed throat to three messages of condolences, two bill collectors, and the last one from an unknown number.

"This message is for Linda Guy Smith. This is Mellon Vending. We have immediate openings for stockers in the Lexington area. The hours are flexible, but you will need to provide your own vehicle. If you're interested, please arrive at our warehouse at 555 Industrial Way no later than nine a.m. Monday morning, prepared to start. Bring a picture I.D."

When the end tone sounded, Linda gave a little laugh. It wasn't the high-powered career she'd hoped for in college, but maybe it would keep the wolf from their door. And right now it was a tiny light of hope to get her through the weekend.

She would take that.

CHAPTER ELEVEN

OCTAVIA STARED UP at the small generic sign that read "Private Investigator" hung over a nondescript door to a lackluster storefront in an uninspiring strip mall on Todds Road that featured a dry cleaner, a pawn shop, a gym, and a Waffle House. "This is it?"

"This is it," Linda said cheerfully.

The kids bailed out of the van and ran inside.

Octavia sagged as all the optimism she'd felt that the agency might be able to find Richard drained away. "I'm guessing Sullivan didn't have a marketing manager."

"I think his philosophy was that people prefer discretion."

She climbed out, her back aching from the cursed futon. At least she was wearing her own clothes and shoes, although she was seriously overdressed for this part of town. "But how did people even find this place?"

"He got referrals...sometimes. The business was still growing."

Because Linda's voice cracked Octavia kept her mouth shut as they walked inside. But it was clear from looking at the dark little hole in the wall that Sullivan Smith had not been running a thriving business. She recalled her conversation with Dunk Duncan, about how he handled only high-end cases. Sullivan was obviously at the other end of that spectrum.

The reception area was small, with dated, dismal wallpaper and an old metal desk with a matchbook under one of the legs. A row of file cabinets lined one wall; random empty drawers stood open. A rickety table held a stack of files. A shredder sat in the floor with strips of mangled paper littering the bad carpet. Packing boxes were stacked nearby.

A woman hugged the children and tweaked their cheeks. Linda introduced her as Klo Calvert, Sullivan's secretary and office manager. Octavia remembered her from the funeral home—her red hair dye was at least three shades too dark and she'd been wearing a skirt much too short for a woman her age. The top she wore today was obviously the rest of that lurid outfit.

"Nice to meet you," Klo said coolly.

"Likewise," Octavia said, trying not to stare at the woman's cleavage. Good God, you could lose a sandwich in there.

While Linda and Klo talked and the kids entertained themselves with a Hacky Sack, Octavia glanced around. Behind the reception area was a small bathroom. To the left was a closed door, which she surmised was Sullivan's office, where he'd collapsed. Linda wouldn't even look in its direction.

"I have a favor to ask," Linda said to Klo. "A background check on an individual—can you do that?"

"Sure. I handled most of the background checks. The fee to the databases we use is paid through the end of the year. I just need a full name and social security number."

When Linda glanced at Octavia, a warm flush climbed her neck. She recited Richard's full name and his social security number.

One of Klo's too-thin eyebrows raised. "Habersham? Are you related to this person?"

"Only by marriage."

"I see."

Octavia hated the knowing look the woman gave her.

"And how deep should I go—credit report? Phone records? Arrest and conviction records?"

She swallowed hard. "The works."

"Are you and he on the same cell phone usage plan?"

"No. His cell phone is through his law firm. But we have a land line at home he sometimes uses."

"Okay, I'll need that number, as well as your social and address." She handed over a pad of paper and a pen. Then she dismissed her by turning back to Linda.

Tingling with embarrassment, Octavia wrote down the information. Damn Richard for putting her in such a demeaning position.

"These are the bills," Klo said in an apologetic voice to Linda, handing over an accordion folder. "I talked to the landlord and unfortunately, if we end the lease early, we'll forfeit a one thousand dollar deposit."

Linda looked stricken, but nodded. "What about receivables?"

Klo shook her head. "None. In fact, we're on the hook to refund some of the retainers clients put down."

"Does the agency have the money?"

"No," the woman said quietly. "But the good news is you'll be able to take a personal tax deduction on the loss the business shows."

Octavia rolled her eyes. As if Linda was going to make enough money stocking vending machines—*gawd*—to pay taxes in the first place. "How many open cases are there?"

Both of the women turned to look at her.

"How many open cases?" she repeated.

"A few," Klo said in a clipped voice.

"Don't you think Linda should see those files?"

Klo bristled. "I was planning to call the clients and let them know we can't complete work on their case."

"Maybe if Linda calls on behalf of her deceased husband, the clients will be less inclined to ask for their retainer back. Ditto with the landlord."

"I don't think—" Linda began.

"No, she's right," Klo said, although she looked as if she didn't appreciate being upstaged. "It could save the business a lot of money, maybe enough to cover the bills."

"Including payroll?" Linda asked.

Klo nodded.

"Then yes," Linda relented with a sigh. "Please make a copy of the open case files. I'll call the clients next week."

"There's one case Sullivan was working on for the D.A.'s office. I already received a phone call asking me to mail the file and his notes to them."

"Of course, send it. I'll come by for the other files before we leave—I need to drop off some thank you notes to the neighboring businesses."

Klo nodded and reached out to clasp Linda's hand. "I can't tell you how sorry—" She broke off and her eyes filled.

"And I'm sorry about your job," Linda said, her eyes welling, too. "What will you do?"

"I usually land on my feet."

Octavia would've guessed the woman usually landed on her back. Irritated at Klo for getting her sister worked up again, she asked, "When will that background check be ready?"

Klo turned flashing eyes in her direction, obviously perturbed at the intrusion by someone she considered an outsider. "Is Monday soon enough?"

"No. But it is what it is," She exchanged a challenging look with the older woman. "Bye now."

When they walked out, Octavia headed toward the van.

"Come with us," Linda said, gesturing to the sidewalk that fronted the motley arrangement of businesses. "After we drop off the thank you cards, we're going to have lunch at the Waffle House."

Octavia made a face. "That's not remotely tempting."

"Waffle House is wonderful," Maggie said with awe in her voice.

Octavia glanced at the little girl's chubby tummy that peeked out under her too-short T-shirt. "Beauty queens shouldn't make a habit of eating waffles."

"Says the woman who packed her a marshmallow lunch," Linda said dryly. Then she gestured with her hand. "Come with us. We could all use a little diversion."

Octavia sighed—how could she argue with that?

Their first stop was a dry cleaner's whose generic sign was as unimaginative as Sullivan's. A chime sounded when they walked in, and they were immediately assailed by heat and the scent of fabric softener. Dust motes floated in the air and the hum of dryers sounded from behind the garment conveyer that was packed with plastic-covered clothes. A slender dark-haired woman emerged from the back and smiled when she recognized Linda. She walked up to the waist high counter, her face pink with perspiration.

"Hello, Mrs. Smith." She was pretty and modestly dressed, and looked to be in her mid-twenties. She spoke with a faint Hispanic accent.

"Hello, Maria." She introduced the woman to Octavia as Maria Munoza.

Octavia didn't extend her hand, but when Maria did, she had no choice except to take it.

"You're Mrs. Smith's sister," Maria said, holding her hand longer than necessary.

"That's right." Octavia squirmed under the woman's coal black eye contact.

The pressure on her fingers increased. "The two of you are very different."

Octavia gave a little laugh. "Right again." And obvious to anyone with vision. She extricated her hand, then took a step back from the disturbing woman.

Linda handed Maria the thank you card. "We just wanted to tell you how much we appreciate you coming to the service and sending flowers."

"You're very welcome. Sullivan was a good man."

A warning bell went off in Octavia's head. How odd that the young woman would call Linda "Mrs. Smith," but call her husband by his given name.

"That's very kind of you to say," Linda murmured.

Maria gave the children each a piece of hard candy, then they were on their way. Octavia felt heat on her back as they were leaving, and when she looked back, the woman was staring at her. She shuddered involuntarily and caught up to Linda and the kids.

The next storefront was empty—not a good indication of the area's prosperity. The next place was called the Slim Gym, a surprisingly spacious facility that seemed to cater to muscle heads, from the sight of the spandex-clad, belt-wearing behemoths doing biceps curls in front of a mirrored wall. Linda warned the children to stay away from the equipment and smiled at the bulky man behind the counter who lit up like neon when he caught sight of her.

Hm.

"Octavia, meet Stone Calvert. He's Klo's nephew and he runs this place. Stone, this is my sister, Octavia Habersham."

The big man with the shaved head had a quiet voice, but a dangerous edge to him. And from the looks of the crude knuckle tattoos, he'd either served in the military, or the penal system—or both. She watched him interact with her sister when Linda handed him the thank you note and caught the whiff of interest on his part. Guys like him and that detective went all Knight in Shining Armor over a widow with kids.

Octavia glanced around. Her personal trainer Javier wouldn't be caught dead in a place like this. She worked out with him twice a week at a club facility that had a sushi bar.

A few sweaty guys went out of their way to walk by her as they picked up a towel or refilled their water bottles from a fountain. One of them flexed his man boob her way.

Ugh—honestly?

As they were leaving, Stone said, "I'm so sorry, Linda. I only wish I could've done more."

"You did plenty," she assured him, "and I'm grateful."

When they left, Octavia quizzed her about the conversation.

Linda made sure the kids were out of earshot, then said, "Stone was the person who found Sullivan and called 9-1-1."

"What was he doing in Sullivan's office?"

"Sully hired Stone sometimes to work cases with him."

Octavia pursed her mouth. She could see how the bald man could be intimidating. So Sullivan took on some dangerous cases, did he? Her estimation of him rose a smidgen.

"When are we getting waffles?" Maggie whined.

"We have one more stop to make first," Linda promised.

Grim's Pawn appeared to be the "anchor" of the sorry little strip mall—at least according to the signage, which was impressive, and the foot traffic, which was steady.

And seedy.

She wrinkled her nose when they stepped inside. Fluorescent lights illuminated every corner. And every square foot of wall space was occupied with junk, as far as she could see. Guitars galore, stereo equipment, televisions, and laptop computers ad nauseum. Glass display cabinets formed a U around the edge of the shop, full of jewelry, coins, and silver pieces. The discards of other people's lives. The place gave her the absolute creeps. She hung back by the door, impatient to leave.

Linda told the children not to touch anything, then waited while a man with his back to them showed a hairy customer a handgun of some kind. Criminals, probably. Derelicts, for sure.

"Aunt Tavey, come look," Maggie said, her voice high with excitement. Octavia walked over to a glass case to see what had her niece so enraptured.

Of course—tiaras.

She crouched to examine them. White, pink, gold, and silver, studded with rhinestones and flowers and colored paste gems, glistening under the lights like the Crown Jewels. Most of them were of inferior quality, but there were some standouts, perhaps college-level pageant awards.

"Aren't they awesome?" Maggie asked, breathless.

"Yes, they are." Octavia wished she could buy the entire case for the little girl. Two days ago, she could've.

Dammit, she hated being poor!

"I see we have a budding Miss America on our hands."

Octavia looked up to see the mocking grin of a dark haired ponytailed man. His arms were covered with colorful—and lewd—tattoos. A memory chord strummed in her head, then she remembered—the ill-mannered thug who'd insinuated himself next to her in the pew at the funeral.

She straightened. "You!"

"Last time I looked."

Her mouth tightened. "I should've known you would run a place like this."

"If you mean profitable, then thank you." He smiled wider. "Linda tells me you're her sister."

Octavia looked across the room to where Linda and Jarrod were perusing musical instruments.

She lifted her chin. "Yes." She gathered Maggie next to her. "And yes, I have no doubt that my niece will someday be Miss America."

"I was talking about you."

She glared. "If you must know, I was Miss Kentucky."

"Were you now? What decade was that?"

Fury rose in her chest. "Of all the insufferable—"

He interrupted her with a laugh. "I'm Grim Hollister. And you are?"

"Leaving," she chirped. "Come along, Maggie."

"Too bad," he said, then nodded to the rear of his shop. "I keep all the good stuff in the back case."

She scoffed "I seriously doubt that you know what 'good stuff' is."

Before she could react, he picked up her hand and squinted at her rings. "I'd say the emerald would make the grade."

Okay, so the plebian knew something about gemstones. The man was probably a thief.

He made a dubious noise. "But he got duped on the sapphire. Matches your eyes, though."

She yanked her hand back. How dare he criticize the jewelry her husband had given her? "Linda," she called, "Maggie and I are heading to lunch."

"We're right behind you," Linda said, pulling Jarrod away.

"Come back sometime," Grim said behind her.

Octavia didn't acknowledge the hoodlum, just kept walking.

Jesus God. How depressing was her life when a waffle was the highlight of her day?

CHAPTER TWELVE

"I NEED SEVEN bags of Doritos and four Clark bars." Linda held out her hand, but when nothing landed in it, she looked over to find Octavia sitting in a chair of the break room on the fourth floor of an office building in which she was not employed.

With her feet propped up on a table.

Eating a Clark bar.

"What are you doing?" Linda hissed.

"My feet are killing me."

"That's why you don't wear four-inch heels to fill vending machines!"

"Filling vending machines is your job, not mine."

"I could've sworn you said you'd help me—you know, in exchange for the whole room and board thing." Linda walked over to a cardboard box and removed the items herself. Her feet hurt, too—along with her entire body, from lifting and squatting and twisting. But she had to keep moving so she didn't have time to stop and think.

About how lousy the weekend had been, sharing space with Octavia and her mountain of clothes.

About how lonely she was now that Sullivan's absence was starting to sink in.

About how desperately she needed this tedious job.

"What building is this?" Octavia asked, gesturing to the nice wood tables and tiled floor. "It's a pretty snazzy break room."

"From all the security we had to go through to get in, I assume it's a government building of some kind. I saw signs for cold check enforcement."

"We should stop by—maybe they have a photo of dear old dad on their wall of fame."

Linda angled her head. "A little help, please? This is our last stop. If we hurry, we can stop by the agency to see what Klo has on that background check."

Octavia's expression went tense, but she lowered her feet. "Okay."

"And stop eating the merchandise."

"I'll pay for it!" Octavia stood and brushed off her dress. After tossing the candy wrapper, she walked back to the box of potato chips and candy bars they'd carried in. "What do you need?"

Linda counted the empty slots in the large springs that delivered the items to the front of the machine and dropped them. "Five Baked Lays, five peanut butter crackers, and three giant cookies."

Octavia rummaged in the box and handed over the items. "This sucks."

Linda fisted her hands and started counting to ten, but only made it to five. "I know. I'm here, too."

"I'm just saying you're too smart and too talented to be doing a job a monkey could do."

"Yeah, well, lucky for me, monkeys don't have to work for a living."

But she knew what Octavia meant. When they were kids struggling together and both dreaming of better days, it hadn't included this particular little scene, of them as grown women, stocking snacks for the grownups who'd actually made something out of themselves.

"If you ask me, I think we should tackle those open cases of Sullivan's."

Linda stared, then gave a little laugh. "That's insane."

"Not really. I looked over the files and they're lame, Nancy Drew-type stuff. You and I can do it."

Linda frowned. "Those files are supposed to be confidential. By all rights, even I shouldn't be looking at them."

"Jesus, Linda, *who* am I going to tell?"

She dismissed the previous ramblings, but Octavia's question seemed to be more deeply rooted. She realized all this time Octavia hadn't been on the phone with friends or neighbors or...anyone. No one seemed particularly concerned about her absence.

Linda forced levity into her voice. "You do have friends, don't you?"

Octavia was suddenly fascinated by the ingredients in a bag of Fritos. "Of course I have friends. At the club. And...all around Louisville. Richard and I do a lot of entertaining."

She allowed the present tense verb to slide by...hopefully Richard was simply on a mental health excursion until their accountant sorted things out. He would probably call Octavia any minute now to smooth things over.

A suited businessman buzzed into the break room and made his way to the coffee machine. While the dark liquid dripped out, his gaze strayed to Octavia.

Her sister was a beautiful woman, Linda acknowledged. Her shoulder-length dark hair and vivid blue eyes were an unusual combination, and her features were sculpted into perfect proportions. Her skin was dark-complexioned and smooth and her lips were full, although she didn't smile nearly enough. Today she was impeccably clad in a red tailored shirtdress and sky-high black heels. With her tasteful and expensive jewelry, her French manicure, and Coach bag, she could easily pass for an executive working in this building.

The ugly Mellon Vending lanyard notwithstanding.

When the man noticed it, his body language changed to dismissive, but it didn't stop him from stealing a glance at Octavia's butt when he left.

"What about you?" Octavia asked.

Linda pushed the final chip-loaded spring back into place, then closed the door to the vending machine and locked it. "What about me?"

"Do you have friends?"

"Sure I do. I have...the neighbors."

"That fat obnoxious lady is your friend?"

"Nan's okay. She's a little nosy, but she means well. Although, I wouldn't call us friends, exactly."

"Then who?"

She picked up one end of the inventory box and waited for Octavia to get the other end before answering. "There are the Logans next door—they have a daughter a couple of years older than Maggie. And I know all the other mothers at school and soccer...most of them, anyway." Linda thought about her tendency to hang back and not get involved in neighborhood activities— the women's walking group, for instance.

At Octavia's dubious look, she felt pressed to further demonstrate her friend-worthiness.

"And there's Klo. She's been like a surrogate grandmother to the children."

"*Hmphh*...she wasn't very friendly to me."

"Maybe that's because you weren't very friendly to her." They moved the unwieldy box toward the elevator. In deference to Octavia's high heels, Linda walked backward and let her sister walk forward.

"What about your two friends from college?"

Linda smiled. "Alisha and Jackie."

"Whatever happened to them?"

"Alisha is a sports agent in L.A., and Jackie is a photographer for *Marie Claire* magazine in Manhattan."

From Octavia's expression, she was thinking the same thing Linda was thinking: her friends had glamorous careers, while she had lots of capri pants.

"Have you seen them lately?"

Linda shook her head. "We exchange Christmas cards. They're both still single...we don't exactly have a lot in common anymore."

"Do they know about Sullivan?"

She nodded. "They both called last week. Alisha couldn't attend the funeral because she was in China with a client. Jackie left a nice voice mail message, said she would visit soon." They had sounded like she felt—worried about her future. And relieved not to be in her shoes. "What about you, are you still friends with anyone from college?"

"I ran into Emmett Kingsley the other day at Sullivan's service. He and I cheered together."

The face of a tall fashionably-dressed man with glasses came to her. "That's who that was! I thought he looked familiar, but there were so many people I didn't get to speak to." Fresh pain stabbed at her—how many people would she never get to thank? "It was nice of him to come. Have you two stayed in touch?"

"Not really." Octavia gave her a wry smile. "I guess growing up, neither one of us got that whole friendship thing down pat, did we?"

"Guess not," Linda conceded. The whole sisterhood thing was still a work in progress, too. She squinted. "There was another man at the service I can't put my finger on—tall, good-looking. I thought I saw you talking to him."

"That was, um, Dunk Duncan."

"Dunk Duncan, the basketball player? That's right—you two used to date."

Octavia's chin went up. "We never dated. He chased me, but I didn't want to be caught."

Linda smiled. That was Octavia, alright—she'd always led men in whatever direction she wanted them to go. Poor girl—this situation with Richard had to be eating at her pride.

They carried the box to the elevator, but a crowd of people were waiting.

"We have to take the stairs," Linda said.

"We'll squeeze in."

"That's one of the rules. We're not supposed to intrude on people going about their business."

"I can't take the stairs in these shoes!"

Linda sighed. "I'll take the box and meet you in the lobby."

"But—"

"Just go." Linda hefted the box out in front of her and wrangled it into the stairwell, which was ten degrees warmer than the rest of the building. She looked over the side and saw the six flights of stairs extending below. At least she was carrying it down instead of up. She proceeded to half-push, half-drag the box down the narrow stairway, knowing with every bump that chips were shattering in their foil bags.

About halfway down Linda sat down on a step to catch her breath. The tears came out of nowhere. She was sweating, her back ached, and *if* she'd done everything right and her accounting sheets were approved when she returned to the warehouse, she stood to make about seventy dollars for the day.

From her big discount clearance purse, she pulled a tissue out of a crushed box of Kleenex and blew her nose. Her phone rang and she managed to dig it out of the bottom.

Oakley Hall.

Her finger hovered over the Talk button. She longed to talk to him, if only to speak with someone who missed Sullivan as much as she did.

But she was still too raw.

She hit the Cancel button to send him to her voice mail.

Linda put away the phone and sniffed mightily. She had to figure out how to get through this mess on her own. She reached into the inventory box, pulled out a Snickers bar and peeled it like a banana. As she chewed, she considering her alternatives, which were slim and few.

And fading fast.

CHAPTER THIRTEEN

OCTAVIA HELD HERSELF against the elevator wall to keep from touching the smelly bodies around her. "There's a thing called deodorant, people."

Glares settled on her, but she didn't care. What a humiliating day, stocking junk food in vending machines, foraging change and dollar bills out of the money boxes like peasants.

Linda couldn't live like this...something had to give.

The elevator doors opened and the crowd surged forward, thank God. She waited until the masses exited, ripped off the dreadful lanyard she'd worn all day, and walked out.

Directly into Dunk Duncan.

He reached out his long arms and caught her as she bounced off his big body. His expression changed from surprise to recognition.

"Octavia! What are you doing here?"

She swallowed her dismay and conjured up a smile while she scanned for Linda. Thankfully, her sister hadn't arrived yet with the telltale box of snacks. "I'm...here with Linda," she said. "Family matters." She discreetly slid the lanyard into her bag.

His handsome face rearranged into concern, then he glanced around. "Where is Linda?"

"We, um, were separated."

"How is she doing?"

Good question. It was clear from her swollen morning eyes that Linda spent the better part of her nights crying, but during the days, she held herself remarkably together. If she were in her sister's shoes, she wouldn't be getting out of bed in the mornings. "Under the circumstances, she's doing okay."

"No woman should have to lose her husband."

Octavia squirmed—or misplace him. "What are you doing here?"

"My office is across the street. I'm here to meet with an assistant D.A. to talk about a case. My agency does a lot of work for the county prosecutor's office."

"That sounds exciting." Damn, but the man could wear a black sport coat.

"Guess I'm still an adrenaline junkie," he said with an easy smile. "This job suits me better than pushing paper."

A jab at her attorney husband, who pushed enough paper to fill the city dump? "So, tell me, Dunk—what makes a good private investigator?"

He pursed his mouth. "A curious mind, good observation skills, and the ability to read people."

"Really?"

"I've always prided myself on knowing what people want before they know it themselves." His voice was rich with innuendo.

Octavia arched an eyebrow. "I thought that was called E.S.P."

He laughed. "Well...some people have accused me of having special powers."

"I'll just bet." Wanting to break away before Linda appeared, she moved toward the door. "I really have to go. It was nice seeing you."

"Are you going to be in town for a while?"

"Maybe," she hedged. "It depends on how long Linda needs me."

"Let's have lunch." He retrieved a business card from his inside jacket pocket and handed it to her.

"I'll have to get back to you." Her pulse blipped when she saw Linda emerge from the stairwell. "Goodbye, Dunk."

"Goodbye, Octavia." He waved and turned toward the elevator, but to her chagrin, he caught sight of Linda and, after doing a double-take, rushed to help her with the box.

She sighed...the man was chivalrous to a fault.

Octavia hurried over to intervene. "Linda, this is Dunk Duncan."

"We were just introducing ourselves," Dunk said. "I explained that Sullivan and I were professional colleagues." He squinted at the cardboard box of potato chips. "Are you...stocking vending machines?" He gave an incredulous little laugh that morphed into the most awkward moment ever.

"Yes, we are," Linda said pointedly.

Dunk looked at Octavia and she wanted to die.

"Oh." He blinked, then recovered. "Well, then...where are you parked? I'll carry this out for you."

"That's not necessary—" Octavia began.

"I insist," he said, then took the box from Linda. "Actually, Mrs. Smith, I wanted to talk to you."

Linda looked wary—good girl. "What is it you want to talk to me about, Mr. Duncan?"

"Call me Dunk."

"Dunk," she relented.

He glanced around at the people zigzagging by them. "Perhaps outside would be more private."

Linda shot Octavia a puzzling look. Octavia lifted her shoulders in the tiniest of shrugs. She followed Linda and Dunk stiffly, wishing she could hit the rewind button for the last five minutes.

Scratch that—make that for the last five *days*.

Dunk kept mum until they reached the minivan and he'd deposited the box inside. Linda thanked him, then waited for whatever he had to say.

He flashed a bullshit smile that encompassed both of them. "I just want to say again how sorry I am for what happened to Sullivan. And I'd like to take any cases he had left open off your hands. His agency would keep the client retainers, of course. Transfer the files to my agency, and we'll simply pick up where he left off."

Warning flags went up in Octavia's head. She had no reason to think he was being anything but magnanimous...and she couldn't imagine what Dunk could possibly gain from taking on Sullivan's leftovers...plus he was offering Linda a tidy way out of her financial dilemma.

Still...Octavia's instincts were screaming that Dunk couldn't be trusted. But it wasn't her decision to make.

Linda offered him a smile. "That's very kind of you to offer, um, Dunk, but we won't be needing your help. Octavia and I will be handling the outstanding cases."

Octavia's eyes bulged, but she had checked herself by the time Dunk swung his surprised gaze her way.

"Really?"

"Really," Octavia confirmed.

He gave a little laugh. "No offense, but what do you girls know about investigating?"

Octavia gritted her teeth because the man had a point.

"Well," Linda said, holding up her Mellon Vending lanyard, "we *girls* know how to get into any building in this city without raising suspicion."

Octavia's jaw dropped. *Go, Linda!*

"But thanks anyway," Linda added.

Clearly perturbed, Dunk had no choice but to retreat. He said goodbye to Linda, and by the time he turned to Octavia, his charm was back. "Call me if you need...anything."

"Will do," she said, and watched him stride away, his long legs eating up the ground. When he was out of earshot, she turned back to Linda. "What was that?"

"I don't know," Linda said, shaking her head. "He was just so damn smug, I couldn't resist."

"You were brilliant...I didn't recognize you."

Linda frowned. "Thanks. I'm still not convinced it's a good idea."

"You and me, working together—how could that go wrong?"

"Right. Get in the van."

Octavia climbed inside, feeling better—meaning less like she was going to have a stroke—than she had since Richard had ditched her at the funeral.

"So," Linda said once they'd pulled onto New Circle Road, heading toward the agency, "is Dunk still chasing you?"

"I get the feeling that Dunk chases a lot of things."

But she couldn't deny that seeing him again gave her a charge. Especially now when her life was not the most inviting place to be. Seeing Dunk reminded her of when she was young and beautiful with countless possibilities scrolling out in front of her.

She pulled out her phone to check for voice messages. When she saw she had one, her heart jumped. Richard? She punched in the number, but it was Frank's voice that came over the line.

"Octavia, I have some bad news about the mortgage. The bank has already taken possession, there's no way to reverse it. You'll need to get everything out that you want in the next couple of weeks, before the locks are changed. There's a chance, of course, that you and Richard could buy it back once the dust settles. Call me when you hear from him. He's still not answering my calls. And, um...there's still the matter of settling my bill."

Octavia deleted the message and closed her eyes. *Richard, where are you?*

"Any news?" Linda asked.

Octavia looked over. "Nothing helpful."

"Maybe Klo will have something."

Octavia nodded, but as they wove through traffic, her apprehension grew. How much did she really want to know about Richard? They had operated as two autonomous units for the better part of ten years. Part of what made them work was allowing the other person to do what they did best...and trusting each other.

She couldn't have misread him all these years.

By the time they'd parked and walked into Sullivan's investigation agency, she had convinced herself it was a wasted exercise. The report would show Richard's credit had cratered, but she already knew that. He obviously hadn't shared with her how much of a hit his firm had taken from the recession, but Richard Habersham was the most straight-laced, uptight, borderline-OCD person she knew. If he was guilty of anything, it was of having too much pride.

Yes...that was all.

They found Klo cleaning out files...and dressed just as inappropriately as before, Octavia noted. Did the woman own a full-length mirror?

"What did you find?" she asked without preamble.

Klo's expression gave away nothing. "Here's everything." She handed over a file folder with a half-inch thick stack of papers inside. "You can sit at my desk," she said, motioning to her chair.

Octavia accepted her offer, relieved when the two women walked away, engrossed in conversation about the open cases, leaving her in relative privacy. Her heart was beating wildly when she opened the file.

But within a few minutes, it had come to a standstill.

Aside from maintaining bank accounts she didn't know about at a bank she wasn't familiar with, last month Richard had bought a handgun.

A handgun? Was this the same man who couldn't even kill his own lobster? The timing of the purchase was too coincidental to ignore.

She had to hand it to Klo—the broad had certainly done her homework. She'd learned the sizable amounts in the bank accounts had been emptied or closed, and the handgun was a 9 mm, whatever that was.

Their home phone records for the past thirty days were listed, along with the name of the person or business calling or being called. Nothing jumped out at her as being suspicious—there were calls from the homeowner's association and the lawn service, and from a cleaning supplies company she didn't recognize. Judging from the short length of the calls, they were either wrong numbers or telemarketers. As expected, there were a few calls from her friends at the club—Joan Berman, Patsy Greenwald, Katie Lender, Renee Masterson. And various calls from creditors, which she now understood.

But she hadn't expected to find anything revealing because Richard conducted most of his personal and professional business over his cell phone.

She almost flipped past the arrest and violations report—Richard was much too law-abiding to do anything untoward, like get a DUI. Which is why she was surprised to see he'd received two unpaid parking tickets in the past few months—proof that he'd had a lot on his mind if he'd allowed those to fall through the cracks.

But it seemed that her meticulous husband had let a lot of things slide lately, including his hold on sanity.

Octavia tried to breathe. While there was a certain amount of relief in knowing that Richard hadn't been kidnapped or worse, was it really better knowing he was AWOL somewhere living on cash he'd made from selling their jewelry and art?

She would argue *no*.

Richard had obviously been planning his escape for a while. But she'd bet he hadn't counted on his wife breaking badass spy.

Octavia closed the file with a smack.

CHAPTER FOURTEEN

KLO HESITATED, her hand on the top file folder on the stack in front of her. "I don't think this is a good idea."

"Yes, you said that already," Octavia offered from the other side of the desk, rolling her hand. "Now let's move on."

Linda looked back and forth between the two women. It was clear they could never work together on a long-term basis. Since Octavia had gotten the background check on Richard yesterday, she'd been more moody than usual. And Klo...well, Linda understood her concern.

"Closing out the open cases is best for everyone," Linda cajoled. "The clients get what they want, and the agency not only gets to keep the retainers, but can collect on the delivery money, too, once the job is done."

Klo looked unconvinced. "But the clients hired Sullivan."

"Sullivan had help—you said yourself that you do the background checks and lots of other things, I'm sure."

Klo nodded.

"And he hired Stone sometimes."

Another nod.

"So the only thing the clients need to know," Octavia cut in, "is that someone on Sullivan's staff is going to take over their case."

Klo looked at her. "What do you know about investigating?"

"I know it's pretty damn antiquated to be using paper files."

"Why don't we discuss the cases," Linda suggested, "and then we can talk about the skills required to finish the jobs."

Klo and Octavia exchanged scowls, but Klo opened the top file folder.

"Case number 10356, Horizons Insurance Company."

Linda found the file and opened it so she and Octavia could share. At the sight of Sullivan's handwriting, she choked up, but pinched herself on the back of her hand to stem the tears.

"A personal injury case and a worker's compensation case," Klo continued. "Basically, the company doesn't want to pay the claims if the employees aren't as injured as they say they are." She gave them a pointed look. "They need proof of the people doing something they're not supposed to be able to do, and they need it fast—by next week. The personal injury case is on contingency— no money shot, no money."

"So we follow them until they do something suspicious, then video them or take a picture?" Linda asked.

"That sounds easy," Octavia said with a scoff.

"Don't be so sure," Klo said. "Some people are professionals at playing the injured party. And you can't invade their privacy to get the picture—it has to be admissible in court."

"Does the agency have a camera with a zoom lens?" Octavia asked.

"Yes."

"Then we got this," she said with a dismissive wave. "Next?"

Klo frowned, then moved to the next file. "Case 10360, Pleasant Ridge Retirement Home."

Linda swapped out the folder and scanned Sullivan's notes. "They have a petty thief inside?"

"Er, not exactly," Klo said. "More like an STD epidemic—gonorrhea, to be specific."

"Excuse me?"

"Ew," Octavia said. "I thought it was an old folks' home."

"Older people have sex," Klo said.

Octavia angled her head. "You *do*?"

"What," Linda interjected while throwing Octavia a stern look, "does the client want, exactly?"

"The owner wants to quietly find patient zero and nip the epidemic in the bud before word gets out to the public."

"How are we supposed to do that?" Octavia asked.

"You're the one who wants to play investigator," Klo said sweetly.

"We'll figure it out," Linda assured them. "What else?"

"Case number 10363, Better Now Convenience Store. The owner thinks one or more of his employees are stealing from him. He needs proof."

A sheet of paper in the file showed the front of the store and a couple of clerks posing for the picture wearing red and yellow striped smocks. "One of us will have to go undercover," Linda asked, then looked at Octavia. "That'll have to be you since I have the vending machine route."

"As long as I don't have to wear that getup."

Klo suddenly looked cheery. "You do, and I'll work out all the details with the owner."

"Meanwhile," Linda said before things got dicey, "Octavia and I have to get going—we'll brainstorm on how we're going to handle the cases."

"I'll be ready in a second," Octavia said, then excused herself to the bathroom.

Klo glanced after her. When the door closed, she looked back to Linda. "Your sister is...interesting."

Linda laughed. "That's putting it mildly. She's having a rough go of things right now."

"And you're not?"

"Yes, of course, but...Octavia is a little less equipped to deal with life's setbacks."

"I hope the background check answered some of her questions?"

"Yes...and raised new ones."

"As is often the case. She's staying with you and the kids for a while?"

"So it seems," Linda said wryly. "It's been bumpy, but I think it's the distraction the kids and I need right now."

"How are the kids?"

She sighed. "They seem to be fine. I talked to their teachers and they haven't noticed any problems. Maggie asks about her dad a lot, is curious about death and heaven. Jarrod is so quiet, it's hard to tell. I think we're all still so bewildered." When she felt the tears coming on again, she forced a smile. "We're muddling through." Then she waved vaguely in the air. "How about things around here?"

"I'm purging files and generally ramping down. Goodwill is going to pick up the office furniture at the end of the month. I'll have some forms for you to sign tomorrow, to close down the business license and the rental agreement on the few pieces of computer equipment we have." She wore a pained expression. "And there are some banking issues to discuss."

Linda's stomach dropped. "Okay. I'll stop by around lunch time."

The woman hesitated, then added, "I'm sure there are some personal things in Sullivan's desk—"

"I'll get to that soon," Linda promised.

Klo nodded, then gestured to the folders Linda held. "By the way, do you have an extra file? I might've accidentally given you the case folder I'm supposed to send to the D.A.'s office. It's labeled 'Foxtrot.'"

Linda checked to make sure the file hadn't inadvertently been mixed in with the others. "No."

"That's odd...I've searched every inch of the office and can't find it anywhere."

Linda darted a glance to Sullivan's closed office door. "Did you check Sullivan's briefcase?"

"Yes, and his desk."

"How about the car he was leasing?"

"I took everything out of it before the dealership picked it up."

"When was the last time you saw the folder?"

"When I first set up the case file. I hate to admit it, but Octavia is right—we should've had our files automated, but Sullivan was very old school, said digital files were too easy for other investigators to hack into. Did he keep any files at home?"

Linda thought of the utter chaos of their house, with building supplies stacked everywhere and her furniture displaced. "No. We were hoping to put an office for him in the den when the renovations were complete." Her throat tightened.

"Don't worry," Klo soothed. "The file will turn up somewhere."

"What did the case concern?"

"I don't know—Sullivan wouldn't tell me anything about it."

"That's unusual, isn't it?"

"Yes, but I assumed A.D.A. Houston had insisted on confidentiality. I didn't push."

Octavia emerged from the restroom, her eyes suspiciously red. Poor Octavia—the day had been one pride-swallowing task after another, from sharing a bathroom at home to counting dirty nickels from the vending machine change buckets.

"Ready?" her sister asked.

Linda felt another pang of sympathy for Octavia, all dressed up in Gucci, but nowhere to go. "Yes." Linda turned to Klo. "I'll let you know if I find the file."

"I'm sure it's here somewhere, just misplaced in the shuffle. See you tomorrow."

She followed Octavia out into the parking lot and headed toward the mini-van. From the sidewalk in front of the pawn shop, Grim Hollister called hello. Linda returned his greeting, but Octavia continued walking rapidly, as if she didn't want anyone to see her at the shabby strip mall.

"Do you mind driving?" Linda asked. "I need to fill out accounting reports before we make our rounds in the morning."

Octavia opened her mouth and Linda expected her to say once again that she didn't drive minivans. Instead she conjured up a smile and held out her hand for the keys. "What file is Klo missing?"

"The case file she's supposed to send to the D.A.'s office."

"Is it a big hairy deal?"

Linda smiled as they climbed inside. "Sounds like it. I knew Sullivan was working on an important case, but I don't know what it was about or who he was working for."

Octavia started up the engine and awkwardly shifted into drive. Linda was sure the dated instruments on the dashboard were a far cry from those of a Jaguar convertible.

"Sullivan didn't talk about his work?" Octavia asked.

"No. It was confidential."

At least that's what she'd told herself. Sullivan said he didn't like to talk about work because he didn't want to bring his job home to affect her and the kids. But some part of her felt as if he purposely excluded her because he wanted to keep something for himself separate from the suburban life thrust upon him. As a result, his job had become like a third person in their marriage, someone she wasn't allowed to get to know.

Which made it all the more ironic that she and Octavia were planning to close out his cases. She realized suddenly that he would not be happy at the prospect.

"So which case do you think we should take on first?" Octavia said, as if she had read her mind. She pulled into traffic on Todds Road in staccato fashion, to the tune of angry horns.

Linda curled her fingers around the armrest. "I'm thinking the personal injury case since it has the biggest potential payout. Tomorrow after we finish the vending route for the week, I have to swing by here and run a couple of errands. So why don't we start Friday?"

"Friday works," Octavia said happily. "Since you have other things to do, I'll do the legwork on the cases."

Linda glanced sideways at her sister. She was being very...accommodating. "You looked upset when you came out of the bathroom earlier. Is everything okay?"

"No," Octavia said, but she was smiling woodenly as she pointed to her forehead. "I spent eight hundred dollars last week to get this wrinkle filled and it's not working because I'm not supposed to frown and that's all I've been doing! Dammit, Richard has the most lousy sense of timing."

Linda smothered a smile. There was the Octavia she knew.

They stopped at the intersection of Man o' War in the right hand turn lane behind a compact car. Linda pulled out the reports she wanted to finish before they got home so she could make dinner and help the kids with their homework. Suddenly, Octavia's head jutted forward.

"That's Richard!"

"Where?"

"In that Mercedes that just drove by!" She lay on the horn. The car in front of her edged forward, trying to make a safe right turn on red to get out of her way.

Octavia rolled down the window and stuck out her head. "Move it!" she yelled, still punching the horn. The car darted out in traffic and Octavia gunned the gas without looking. Screeching brakes and more horns sounded.

Linda's paperwork went flying. "Jesus, sis, you're going to get us killed."

Octavia zoomed around cars, then pointed. "There it is! The black one."

Linda squinted to see a vehicle about a quarter of a mile in front of them on the busy two-lane road. "Are you sure it's Richard? Did you see him?"

Octavia floored the pedal and ran through a yellow-turning-red light. "No, but that's his car."

"Slow down—it could be anyone."

"But it could be him."

She was right. Linda glanced in the side mirror to see what kind of carnage Octavia had left in her wake and at the sight of flashing blue lights, her stomach dropped to her thighs. "Pull over, sis. You've got a cop behind you."

"I can't stop—I'll lose him!"

"You *have* to stop—it's the law."

Octavia cursed, but backed off the gas pedal. She migrated into the right lane, then eased onto the shoulder. The dark police car pulled in behind her. Linda said a quick prayer that her car insurance was paid up. This could be bad.

Octavia had rolled down the window and was fluffing her hair.

"What are you doing?"

"Getting out of a ticket," she said, then unfastened the top two buttons on her blouse.

The cop's face appeared in the window. "What the hell—" He broke off. "Octavia?"

Linda gasped. "Oakley?"

He frowned. "Well, at least you're not driving." Then he scowled at Octavia. "Do you know how fast you were going?"

"You were driving just as fast to catch up with me."

Linda closed her eyes briefly.

"The difference is I'm allowed to! What were you thinking? The children just lost their father—are you trying to kill their mother, too?"

"Oakley—" Linda began.

"License and registration," he said.

Octavia gaped at him. "You're giving me a ticket?"

"You better believe it. You broke about a half dozen traffic rules."

Octavia's mouth screwed up, but she reached for her purse.

Linda rummaged in the van glove compartment around toys and crayons for the registration, which she passed over. "Since when do detectives work the traffic beat?"

A muscle ticked in his jaw. "Since maniac drivers threaten the safety of people I care about."

She pursed her mouth. "Can we talk?"

"You're welcome to come back to the car while I write up this ticket."

She climbed out into deep grass, then waded back to his unmarked sedan and slid inside, feeling like a naughty child.

He swung into the driver's seat, his body language vibrating with anger.

"Oakley, let me explain. Octavia's husband left her here the day of the funeral. He just up and disappeared, and since then she's found out they're deeply in debt and he was doing things she didn't know about. She thought she saw him drive by and was following him. I know it's not a good excuse for speeding, but there it is."

He was quiet for a few seconds. "No, it's not a good excuse. What's the guy's name?"

"Richard Habersham. He's an attorney in Jefferson County. Is there anything you can do?"

"It's not illegal to disappear....but I'll keep my eyes open in case anything about him comes over the wire."

"So can you cut her some slack?"

"No—she's getting a ticket. She's very lucky no one was hurt." His shoulders softened a millimeter. "How are you doing?"

I have a stone where my heart used to be. "Some days are better than others."

"Did you get my messages?"

She nodded. "I've just been so busy with the kids and Octavia...and closing down the agency."

He reached forward to lift the ugly Mellon Vending lanyard she wore around her neck. "What's this?"

"I...got a part-time job."

His face clouded.

"I'd planned to...even before." Although Sullivan had never known.

"Surely there's something else..."

"It's not a bad job. The hours are flexible enough for me to work around the kids' school schedule."

He reached into his inside coat pocket and removed his wallet. "Take this—" He pulled out several hundreds and extended them to her.

Her mouth watered, thinking of the bills she could pay, but she didn't want to take money from Oakley, didn't want things to get...sticky. "I can't."

"I insist."

She put her hands in her pockets.

Finally he put the money back. "How are the kids?"

"They miss their dad. And so do I."

He nodded. "Me, too."

When the silence became uncomfortable, he cleared his throat, then continued writing the ticket. "Don't let your sister be a bad influence on you."

"Maybe I'll be a good influence on *her*."

He laughed, the tension broken. "Don't be a stranger, okay?"

"Okay."

She climbed out and returned to the van.

"Did you talk him out of it?" Octavia asked.

"No."

"No? I thought he was a friend of yours."

Oakley appeared at the window. "But I'm not a friend of *yours*." He tore off the ticket and handed it to her. "While you're in Lexington, please obey the law."

Octavia snatched the ticket.

"Goodbye, ladies. Be safe."

He disappeared and instantly, Linda missed him.

CHAPTER FIFTEEN

"WELCOME TO Waffle House. What can I get you for?"

Octavia looked up, straining not to roll her eyes. She had to consider her surroundings—she was, after all, sitting in a sticky booth with large containers of condiments right on the table, and the boy waiting on her wore an apron and a black bill cap with WH embroidered on the front.

A bill cap.

"Coffee, with half and half."

"Coming right up."

Octavia looked back to the file she was studying, the background report on Richard. She was systematically going through all the information and drawing a line through all the facts she'd known to highlight the facts she hadn't known.

So far, *hadn't* was winning.

The boy came back and set an enormous mug of coffee on the table. "Whoa, whatcha doing there? Studying for an exam?"

"No." She took a sip of the coffee and conceded it wasn't bad.

"Nice phone," the boy said, nodding to her smartphone lying on the table.

She prided herself on having the latest model...even if she didn't know how to use it fully. "Thanks."

"Do you have the Go Man app?"

"No." At least she didn't think so. She had no idea what the boy was talking about.

"I can show you sometime—it's cool."

"I'll keep that in mind."

"Are you going to order something to eat?"

She *was* hungry, darn it. "What's the safest thing on the menu?"

"For lunch, a lot of people like you order the Chicken Apple Pecan Salad."

Octavia frowned. "People like me?"

"Thin and pretty."

"Oh...thanks. Okay, I'll try it."

"You got it."

She picked up her phone and went down a list of her and Richard's friends, dialing...but most of them wouldn't take her calls. She got lots of voice mailboxes, and secretaries and housekeepers and personal assistants whose bosses had "just stepped out." Of the people who *would* take her calls, no one had heard from Richard in days. But the gossip had started to churn.

"Is everything okay, Octavia?" Emily Devonshire asked. "Someone said Richard had closed his practice..."

"...that your home had been foreclosed upon," said Joan Berman.

"...that your cars were repossessed," said Katie Lender.

"...that your housekeeper is looking for another job," said Renee Masterson.

"Everything is fine," Octavia lied to each of them with a laugh. "I'm in Lexington with my sister—she lost her husband, you know, so sad—and Richard decided to take a break, too. But in all the flurry, I lost his itinerary, so I thought maybe one of our friends would know where he went. And the financial stuff—well, we rely on our CPA for everything, and obviously, something fell through the cracks. You just can't get good help these days."

But each of her friends made lame excuses to get off the phone, leaving her stung. How quickly the sharks could turn on their own when they smelled blood in the water.

She pulled from her purse the handful of mail she'd grabbed on her way out the door of her home, and the padded envelope Carla had given her fell into her lap. She picked it up and studied the flap—whatever was inside, Richard had gone to great lengths to document that he was the person who'd sealed the envelope. She knew an evidence envelope when she saw it, and knew if it was something damning, she didn't want to be the one responsible for breaking the seal. Richard must be keeping it for a client.

But why would he give it to Carla?

The truth hit her between the eyes—because he'd been sleeping with her, of course.

"Octavia, right?"

She looked up to see Grim Hollister standing there, clad in black jeans, black T-shirt, and white snakeskin boots. She frowned and put a finger to the crease in her brow. "Don't talk to me."

"Having a bad day, huh?"

"That's so none of your business."

"There aren't any free tables—mind if I join you?"

"Yes, I do."

He slid into the booth seat opposite her. "Thank you kindly. You're here alone?"

She gritted her teeth. "My sister is taking care of some things at the agency."

The waiter arrived with her salad. Octavia moved her files and mail to make room for the bowl. Damn, it looked kind of good.

"Hey, Grim," the waiter said.

"Hey, Brittany."

"Your usual?"

"Sure thing."

"Coming right up."

Octavia turned to stare after the server. "That's a girl?"

"Yeah...kind of hard to tell, isn't it? Smart as a whip, that one. But she doesn't make a fuss like you do."

"You can leave now."

Instead, he leaned back in the seat and crossed his big tatted arms. "I like women who fuss."

"How charming."

"Dig in," he said, nodding to her salad. "Don't feel like you have to wait for me."

"I don't." She stabbed her fork into a chunk of chicken.

"Come here often?"

"Do I look like I belong in here?"

He angled his head. "I can see it—you haven't always been rich, have you?"

Jackass. She stabbed another chunk and brought it to her mouth for a vicious tear.

He squinted at the paperwork she'd moved aside. "Background check, huh?"

Rankled, she reached over to close the file that contained the report on Richard.

"I do them all the time in my business," he offered. "For gun purchases."

She took her time chewing and swallowing. "I don't care."

"So, what do you do for a living, Octavia?"

"I'm not employed."

"Not to be confused with being unemployed. Lucky you—hubby must make a boatload—you have some nice jewelry."

Her blood pressure bumped higher, but she realized if she continued to engage with him, he'd never go away. She kept eating.

From her stack of mail, he picked up a Rolex brochure. "Are you in the market for a new watch?"

She took another bite.

"I can set you up, got a nice selection of ladies' gold timepieces."

She swallowed, then took a long drink of coffee. Time to set the peddler straight. "I don't buy my jewelry in pawn shops."

"Too bad—you could save a lot of money. Or buy twice as much."

"You're missing the point."

"No, I get it—you'd rather pay for the privilege of going to a big jewelry store in the mall where your friends will see you."

"Here ya go, Grim," Brittany said, setting a bulging brown paper bag on the table.

"Thanks, doll." He handed her a twenty. "Keep the change."

"Thanks, man." She crammed the money into her apron, then turned to Octavia. "How's the salad?"

"The salad's fine," Octavia said, then glared at Grim. "It's the company that's lacking."

He smiled up at Brittany. "She hasn't warmed up to me yet. Hey, I got a vintage Atari game console in the shop yesterday. Want me to hold it so you can take a look?"

Brittany's eyes lit with interest, then she bit her lip with dainty white teeth. "Can I afford it?"

"We'll work out a trade...my desktop is running kind of slow, probably needs a tuneup."

She grinned. "Easy peasy."

"Stop by after work if you have time."

"Will do." The girl scooted away.

Octavia smirked. "Kind of young for you, don't you think?"

He sobered. "She's sixteen, no mom, and her dad doesn't know she exists."

She knew a little about that. "And you're some kind of savior?"

"Nope...just someone who gives a damn."

The man was infuriatingly self-righteous. "When you get down from your cross, feel free to go."

He picked up the bag and stood, then leaned down. "You'd be a knockout if not for that frown wrinkle between your pretty blue eyes."

Without breaking eye contact, Octavia picked up the giant container of ketchup from the table, turned it over, and squirted a big blob over his white snakeskin boots. She knew enough about exotic skins to know snake was absorbent.

He looked down at his boots. "That wasn't nice."

"I'm not a nice person."

"I'm beginning to notice." He straightened, then turned and walked out of the restaurant.

Ugh, galling man. But then, weren't they all? She stared at the padded envelope and envisioned Richard slipping it to Carla when they were in bed... God, had they done it in her own house...in her own bed?

Angry tears filled her eyes, but she refused to let them fall. It was difficult to picture Richard with another woman—his sex drive was not particularly high...a common phenomenon of successful men, she'd discovered as her friends from the club had lamented their husbands' lackluster performance in the sack.

But why else would he give the envelope to Carla?

More humiliating than her husband humping the maid...did anyone else know about it?

Of course they did...men couldn't help themselves—they had to brag to their friends. And then the men told their wives...

Which explained why everyone was avoiding her.

She picked up her phone and dialed Carla's phone number, but got her voicemail. "Carla, this is Mrs. Habersham. I know what's going on between you and my husband, you little tramp! Call me back if you know what's good for you."

She sat back, soaking in misery and sending laser beams of hate toward Richard wherever the fig he was. Then she turned back to the mail, hoping to find a stray stock dividend check or tax refund. But it was only bills, bills, bills, an invitation to a club dinner next Wednesday, notice of a charity fundraiser Botox party—how passé—wait....

Octavia went back to the club dinner invitation and a plan oozed into her head. She smiled to herself. What an excellent opportunity to confront everyone at once to find out what they knew about her husband.

CHAPTER SIXTEEN

"DO YOU SEE him?" Octavia asked.

"No," Linda said, binoculars to her face. "Just like the last time you asked twenty seconds ago."

"Are you sure? Someone has to be home, there's smoke coming out of the chimney."

"Um, I think that's exhaust coming out of the dryer vent."

"Whatever."

"I'm telling you, I don't see anything."

"Scan the top floor windows where the bedrooms are probably located— we might catch him in the act."

"In the act of what?"

"Having sex."

"Oh, that's nice."

"It'll make our case," Octavia insisted, reading from the file. "According to Mr. Wendt's medical claim, the injury he sustained when he fell off a ladder and hurt his back makes it impossible for him to walk without aid, or get an erection."

Linda lowered the binoculars she had aimed at the blue house across the street. "It's also illegal to photograph someone having sex in a private place. I thought you were going to do the legwork."

"This is my first case!"

"This is *my* first case, too, but I know the Peeping Tom law."

"I forgot—you're one of those by-the-book people."

Linda poked her tongue into her cheek. "Why does the insurance company think he's lying?"

"Because this is his third personal injury claim with his third employer in as many years."

"Which means he's probably good at this."

"He's a man, which automatically means he's a liar." Octavia took the binoculars and lifted them to her face. "It just remains to be seen if he's lying about his back. And his dick."

That lying sentiment had been close to the surface. "No word from Richard, huh?"

"Nope. But I have reason to believe he's having an affair."

Linda turned her head, but her sister didn't move, simply held the binoculars to her face as if she'd just announced that she'd had eggs for breakfast.

"I'm so sorry, sis. Are you sure?"

"Why else would he have taken off, if not for another woman?"

"But to leave his practice, too?"

Octavia shrugged. "Things were closing in on him. I think for some men, it's just easier to walk away from everything and start over than to stay and fix the things they broke."

Linda didn't have any advice...not when she herself had been entertaining thoughts of starting fresh the very day Sullivan had died. Her cheeks burned at the memory of her selfish fantasies.

"Remind me," Octavia said. "What did Mr. Wendt do for a living?"

Linda picked up the folder. "It says here that he stocked groceries."

"That doesn't seem like a particularly dangerous job."

"Lots of twisting and lifting, I suppose...and he allegedly fell off a step ladder."

Octavia scoffed. "*I've* fallen off a step ladder."

Linda squinted. "When?"

"Well, not me, but my maid Carla has...and she bounced right back up. Of course, I've come to understand that bouncing might be a talent of hers."

She cringed—so Richard had slept with the housekeeper. How humiliating for Octavia.

"Does it say how long Sullivan had Wendt under surveillance?"

She flipped through the pages in the file to scan his scrawled notes. Sullivan had not been a scholar—spelling and penmanship were not his strong suit. "Looks like three weeks." Her heart pinched. He must've been desperate for that money-shot payoff. Had she nagged him about money? Had the stress over money triggered his heart attack?

She kept reading, deciphering. "In his notes, Sullivan wrote that he observed several women going in and out of the house, women who appeared to be prostitutes. He questioned the women, but none of them would admit to having sex with Wendt, they all claimed to be taking care of him or his house."

"So he *is* lying about his dick."

Linda bit her lip. She was aware Sullivan came into contact with some unsavory characters in his line of work, but knowing he'd questioned hookers left her feeling a little...frumpy. And embarrassed that he'd had to come home to her in her mom jeans and Hamburger Helper.

Had he hated his life?

Octavia lapsed into silence and Linda maintained it, marinating in regret. They both had a lot on their minds, it seemed.

Minutes ticked off the clock in the dashboard that predated digital displays. After some time, Octavia lowered the binoculars with a labored sigh. "This is excruciating."

Linda had to agree. They'd been sitting parked in a line of cars across the street from Mr. Wendt's house for almost two hours without a sighting. She was hungry and she needed to pee. She shifted her legs that were sweating against the seat. "Welcome to the world of private investigating."

"*Ugh*—where's the ah-ha moment, the car chase?"

"I think we've had enough car chases," Linda reminded her. Oakley's concern came back to her...he also would not approve of her taking over Sullivan's cases.

In fact, Octavia was the only person who thought she was capable of it.

But did that make them both crazy?

"Wait—someone's coming out."

Linda picked up the zoom-lens camera and focused on the front door. It opened and a man emerged in a motorized scooter.

"That's him," Octavia said. "I thought he was in a wheelchair."

"He must've upgraded." Linda took a couple of photos for practice—and to establish a timeline. Mr. Wendt was a regular looking man, neat and attractive—nothing about him screamed criminal. He held an envelope and buzzed toward the mailbox at the end of the driveway.

He tried to position himself close enough to open the hinged door, but couldn't quite reach. Linda snapped more photos.

"Go ahead, get up and do a jig," Octavia muttered.

But he kept straining and stretching from his seated position until he finally opened the mailbox, put the envelope inside, and raised the flag.

Both of the women groaned in defeat.

Then something in the street caught Mr. Wendt's attention. For a few seconds, Linda was afraid he was going to look their way. But whatever it was, it was lying on the ground.

"It's a bill," Octavia said. "I can't tell what denomination."

"Let's hope it's a hundred," Linda said.

He looked both ways in the street, then buzzed over to the money and leaned down. No matter how far he stretched, though, the bill was just beyond the grasp of his fingers.

"Come on, stand up," Octavia muttered. "Linda, are you getting this?"

"Yes."

Suddenly the man's head swung around and his eyes widened. A car was barreling straight for him. He yelled and waved his arms, then put his scooter in reverse, but he wasn't moving fast enough. The women both held their breath until the car screeched to a stop in front of him. Then Wendt turned around and puttered back to the sidewalk.

They exhaled.

"Well, that's it," Linda said. "If the man didn't stand up and run to get out of the way of a moving car, he can't stand up."

Octavia pursed her mouth. "Unless he knows someone is watching and he staged the whole thing."

"That's pretty elaborate, don't you think?"

"Klo said some of these people are professionals. What's a few dollars to hire a buddy to nearly run you down if it helps you collect a million bucks in a personal injury case?"

Linda shook her head. "I just can't believe people would be so..."

"Bad?"

"Yeah."

"Well, believe it. Not everyone is like you, Linda."

She said it as if that was a good thing. Linda let the remark slide because she knew her sister was hurting over her husband's betrayal, despite her gruff exterior.

They were deflated, expecting Wendt to head back inside, but instead he turned the scooter around and motored off in the opposite direction.

"Where do you think he's headed?" Octavia asked.

"I don't know, but I'll have to follow him at a good distance, or he'll spot us for sure."

Thirty minutes later, they were still following him, driving at less than ten miles an hour as he traveled from road to road via sidewalks and crosswalks. When he turned onto Nicholasville Road, a major road with serious traffic, Linda stuck out her arm and waved yet another car around them.

"You got your car chase," she remarked dryly.

"This is ridiculous. Who knows where he's going."

"Probably to the Fayette Mall. It's only another half mile or so."

Sure enough, eventually the man puttered into the mall parking lot and headed for the main entrance.

Linda hung back, then found a parking place. Octavia tucked the camera into her designer bag and straightened her clothing—a silky coral-colored button-up blouse and a slim black skirt with sandals. Next to her, Linda felt like Suburban Mom, minus the cape.

Inside, they located Mr. Wendt quickly—he was hard to miss in his scooter. They maintained a discreet distance, pretending to shop. Octavia wandered into a jewelry store and tried on a diamond Rolex watch with a price tag that took Linda's breath away. The look in her sister's eyes reminded her of when their father had brought home the pony.

And the look in her eyes when she had to take it off reminded Linda of when the pony had been spirited away.

Wendt visited a bookstore where he waited for ten minutes to request assistance to see a book on a top shelf. Then he went into an electronics store to buy a battery for his scooter—he obviously planned to be in it for a while. Next he went to Macy's department store where he touched every pair of socks in the men's hosiery department while she and Octavia loitered nearby, trying to look casual.

Linda glanced at her watch. "I have to go in twenty minutes to be home when the kids get there."

Octavia scowled after their target, who had finished fondling accessories and was zooming back out into the center of the mall. "I have an idea." She handed her purse to Linda. "Get the camera ready, and whatever happens, go with it."

A phrase that never failed to strike fear in her heart when they were kids... and still had the same effect.

Linda had no choice but to scamper after Octavia, who strode after Wendt and when she caught up with him, bumped his scooter—hard. So hard that it tipped over and spilled him out into the smooth, slick floor.

Linda watched in horror as the man flailed on his back, reaching futilely for his toppled scooter.

"Step back," Octavia shouted when people approached to help him. "This man is a con artist, he's as able to walk as you or I." Then she smiled down at Wendt. "Get up, you big phony."

Linda closed her eyes. Octavia had gone way too far. She'd be lucky if she wasn't arrested for assault.

Wendt lay there and shook his head. "You're crazy! I'm paralyzed—I can't get up."

Her sister crouched over him. "Really? Can you get *it* up?" She began unbuttoning her blouse, revealing a black bra underneath.

Linda stood riveted with the rest of the crowd as Octavia removed her blouse, then stepped out of her skirt. She stood over Wendt in lacy bra and panties and high heels as catcalls sounded in the background and mothers covered the eyes of their children.

Wendt was transfixed.

"Ladies and gentlemen," Octavia said triumphantly, pointing to his crotch. "We have lift-off."

Linda stepped forward to snap a picture of Wendt and his painfully obvious erection just as mall security came running up.

Octavia held them off with an upraised hand, and apparently, they were too disoriented by her state of undress to disobey. "Are you going to get up now?" she asked Wendt.

His mouth opened and closed as he took in Octavia's barely concealed curves.

Linda felt sorry for the man—the photo of his obvious arousal would be enough to dispute part of his claim...they didn't need to mock his inability to walk.

"Octavia," Linda hissed. "We have what we need. Let's go."

Then Wendt rolled over and pushed to his feet. "Okay, you got me. Can I at least have your number?"

CHAPTER SEVENTEEN

"WHEN WILL MOMMY be home?" Maggie whined.

"If she's like me, when she runs out of room in the car for shopping bags," Octavia said. She was trying to figure out how to work the ancient vacuum cleaner. There was a reason she had a housekeeper.

"Mom's nothing like you," Jarrod blurted from the couch where he sat watching something loud on TV that looked inappropriate.

She walked over and turned the channel to Saturday morning cartoons, then put the remote out of reach. He flounced, but she only offered a tight smile, then went back to the vacuum.

"When are you and your stuff leaving?" he asked, jerking his thumb toward the bags of clothes and shoes stacked all over the room.

"As soon as we possibly can. You don't think I *want* to be here, do you?"

"Can I have these shoes?" Maggie asked. She stood posed, with her chunky little feet inside a pair of cotton candy pink stilettos, looking hopeful.

"Someday. For now, stay out of my shoes—you'll break the shank."

"What's a shank?"

"The thing you'll break if you don't take them off!"

"It's on the side," Jarrod said.

She sighed. "What?"

"The button to turn on the vacuum. It's on the side." Then he got up and reached for it. "Here, I'll do it."

"Good," she said, happily relinquishing the monster.

"It's not going to make a difference," he mumbled, eyeing the general disarray of the house.

"I know...I have eyeballs."

The doorbell rang and Max began barking at the top of his lungs.

"I heard it!" she shouted to the dog, then walked to the door thinking her head might explode. How did Linda deal with this unrelenting chaos day in and day out?

She opened the door to find a brown-suited delivery man. "Package for Mrs. Smith."

"What is it?"

He checked the manifest. "A case of battery-operated candles." He grinned. "She gets the most interesting things."

She squinted, begging to differ. But she signed for it as he dragged the box inside and somehow found a place to set it. She thanked him and when he left, she walked out into the front yard to fetch the newspapers that had piled up near the stoop.

It was a too-hot morning, with gnats buzzing around her head. On the broken sidewalk in front of the house a couple dressed in ill-fitting clothes were walking a yappy little dog. They smiled and waved. She stared at them because they seemed so happy...who could be happy living in this shabby little community?

Didn't they know they were supposed to be depressed?

"Looks like your yard is getting away from you," the man called good-naturedly.

Linda's sloping yard was indeed overgrown, as many weeds as grass, and nearly consumed by clover. And apparently its appearance was bringing down the entire neighborhood.

"I'll get the gardener right on that," Octavia called, then gave him the finger.

The couple's jaws dropped, then they hurried on their way.

A blue sedan pulled up next to the sidewalk and a stocky blond man emerged from the passenger side dressed in a suit. Everything about him was out of place, but in the back of her mind she wondered if he were a cop, maybe a former colleague of Sullivan's. But he made a beeline for her, as if he knew who she was. Before she realized what was happening, he grabbed her upper arm.

"Where's Richard?"

Fear catapulted through her at his ominous expression.

He shook her. *"Where is he?"*

"I...I don't know," she managed.

Another shake, this one rattling her teeth. "I think you do."

From the corner of her eye she saw a reddish-brown streak fly past her. Max was on the man's leg, his teeth buried in the fabric of his pants.

"Leave my Aunt Tavey alone!" Maggie shouted from the stoop.

"Hey, you," Jarrod yelled.

The man looked up just as a basketball hit him square in the nose. He grimaced and released Octavia to hold his gushing nose. While he groaned and cursed, Maggie ran up and threw a cup of glitter on him.

"You're a bad man!"

The bad man clawed at the air to rid himself of the sparkly bits, to no avail. But apparently he'd had enough because he turned and ran back to the car, holding his nose. Max pursued part of the way, barking a noisy sendoff. The man rolled inside, then the car sped off. Octavia saw a few letters and numbers on the license plate and committed them to memory.

She turned to look at the kids, who were staring at her, wide-eyed. "Are you okay?" she asked, hugging them close. She would never forgive herself if something happened to them on her watch.

"We're fine," Jarrod said. "Did that man hurt you?"

"No," she said, although her arm still stung from his bruising grip. "Thanks to you—you guys are my heroes!"

"And Max, too," Maggie said.

"And Max, too," Octavia agreed, giving the dog a tentative pat on the head.

"Why did that man come here?" Jarrod asked. He looked wary, as if he were afraid the guy might come back.

"He was looking for someone," she said evasively. "But he had the wrong house." She made a shooing motion, forcing cheer into her voice. "Let's all go back inside."

But when she closed the door, she turned the deadbolt. Adrenaline still coursed through her body. The man was obviously trying to find Richard, and from his demeanor, she gathered it wasn't to give him money. The handgun purchase listed on Richard's background check was starting to make sense.

Who had her husband gotten himself mixed up with?

"Kids," she said when she turned around, "let's not tell your mom what happened."

"Why not?" Jarrod asked.

"Because it might upset her needlessly. And she has enough on her mind, don't you think?"

He nodded and looked at Maggie. "We won't tell."

"It'll be our secret," Maggie agreed in a hushed voice, then crossed her heart.

"Good," Octavia said, relieved. "Now...who wants pancakes?"

———

Linda reached down to lift a spider chrysanthemum from the mound of dying flowers covering Sullivan's grave. The white bloom, amazingly, was still alive after ten days.

Her eyes filled with tears and overflowed again, still unable to get her head around the idea that her husband was in the ground, feeling nothing. She'd come here to talk to him, to feel close to him, but she didn't know what to say. His life had been so brief, and she wasn't even sure he'd been happy.

From the box of Kleenex she'd brought with her, Linda pulled yet another tissue and wiped her face. In a tragically short amount of time, the boxes she'd won were dwindling. All of her pockets and purses were full of crumpled balls and moist wads.

"The kids are okay," she started. "As good as they can be. They miss you so much."

The echoing silence that answered her permeated bone deep.

She swallowed. "Octavia is staying with us for a while." She gave a little laugh. "I know—can you imagine? She's not acclimating well...and she and Maggie are so much alike, it's unending drama as to which one of them is queen bee. But I think it's just what we all need right now."

She wet her lips. "Oakley is keeping an eye on us. He misses you." Her neck warmed and she squirmed—it was as if she could feel Sullivan's disapproval from beyond.

"And in case it matters," she whispered, "I miss you, too." At a loss, she dropped the mum onto his grave and turned to walk away.

CHAPTER EIGHTEEN

LINDA TURNED HER head to study Octavia's profile. "You were quiet all weekend. Is everything okay?"

Octavia didn't move, just kept staring blindly ahead out the windshield of the van. "You mean other than the fact that my husband has disappeared and I don't know what I'm going to do?"

"Ditto," Linda said softly.

Octavia looked over and shifted in her seat. "I'm sorry...I realize you're struggling, too."

"You know you can stay with us as long as you want to."

"I appreciate that, but you have your life, and I really need to get back to mine. Which reminds me—can I borrow the van Wednesday after we finish the vending machine route? I need to make a trip back to Louisville to pick up a few things."

"Sure." Linda bit her lower lip. She hadn't really expected Octavia to enjoy living in her cramped household, sharing her small life. And of course she was pining for her husband and the lavish lifestyle she'd had in Louisville, but...Linda was sort of getting used to having her sister around again, and it was...nice.

Octavia picked up the Pleasant Ridge Retirement Home file from her lap, suddenly all business. "Okay, how are we going to do this?"

"Well, the owner doesn't want everyone in the home to panic about the outbreak, so while we don't have to go in undercover, we're supposed to handle our inquiries with discretion." She gave Octavia a pointed look. "And without stripping down to our skivvies."

"Hey, it worked, didn't it? Wendt folded like a greeting card."

"But what if he hadn't?"

"I figured we had nothing to lose—if it worked, great. If it didn't, then the insurance company was going to have to pay him anyway."

"What if he'd had a bad back and you'd hurt him worse?"

"But he didn't...and I didn't."

"We could've lost a big customer."

Octavia frowned. "The insurance company? What does it matter? You're closing the agency."

"Right," she murmured. "You're right, of course."

"And we're collecting a big, fat payment. You're welcome, by the damn way."

"No, I do appreciate it. God knows we can use the money."

"Can't we all."

She'd promised Octavia half of the payment, although Klo said it would take a few weeks to arrive.

By that time, Octavia would probably be back in Louisville.

"We have the names of three residents who came forward to be treated," Linda said. "They've agreed to talk to us, but we'll probably have to conduct a lot of other interviews. So how *are* we supposed to strike up a discreet conversation with a group of elderly people about their sex lives without arousing suspicion?"

"We could tell the residents we're senior matchmakers."

Linda pursed her mouth. "Not bad...I think we can make that work."

They agreed on the pieces of information they would need from each resident they spoke to, but Octavia remained detached. Linda pulled into the parking lot of the retirement home and edged the van into an empty spot. She wished she knew what was bothering her sister, although she acknowledged Octavia had plenty on her plate to worry about. Still, she preferred sarcasm over this quiet sullenness.

As they walked through the lobby, clusters of elderly people passed them, all at different stages of activity, but most of them spry. The majority were women who obviously enjoyed dressing up and looking their best. Lots of waves and smiles came their way.

"Looks like a friendly place."

"We have medical proof of that," Octavia said dryly. "Ugh, I positively refuse to get old."

Linda had to agree that getting old didn't have the same appeal as when she'd assumed she and Sullivan would age together. "If anyone can fend off Mother Nature, I'm sure you can."

They walked up to a reception area that resembled a hotel reservations desk.

"May I help you?" a young man asked.

Octavia dazzled the handsome clerk with a smile. "Linda and Octavia Guy—we should be on the visitor list."

Linda shot her a surprised glance. Octavia had given Klo their maiden name to use?

"Here you are," the man agreed. "It says you're guests of the owner."

"That's right. We're here to take a tour of the place."

"Oh, good. Are you looking for housing for a parent?"

"Yes—our mother."

Linda managed to conceal her shock—Octavia never mentioned their mother. *Never.*

"Is your mother with you?"

"No—she's out of town."

Linda held her breath—that much was true. Where, however, was anyone's guess.

"Okay. Let me call our director—she'll want to escort you around."

"What's your name?"

"Tyson Gilly, ma'am."

"Save the ma'am for your mother, Tyson. I'm just Octavia."

His face turned bright red. "Yes, ma'am—er...Octavia."

"Tyson, we're kind of in a hurry, and we really don't want to bother the director. So we're going to take one of these nifty maps and walk around, ask the residents a few questions, and be gone before you know it. Okay?"

"I guess that would be okay...Octavia."

Linda wiped away a smile with her hand. When Octavia wanted to, she could charm a male zebra out of his stripes.

Octavia winked at him. "We'll be back before you know it."

He straightened. "I'm counting on it."

Another heart bites the dust, Linda thought wryly.

As they walked away, Octavia handed her a map. "I got one for you, too. I figure we can cover twice as much ground if we split up. I'll take the east wing and the activity center, you take the west wing and the dining room. Let's find out who these horny old gals have been sleeping with and meet back here in forty-five minutes. Ready?"

Linda blinked. Her sister had obviously missed her calling. "Okay."

———

Octavia bit into a chicken finger and studied the UK dry erase board where Linda had diagramed all of their conversations from the retirement home with a decision tree.

Her sister had obviously missed her calling.

"I've color coded red all the residents who came forward to say they had the STD."

"What's an STD?" Jarrod asked. They were all sitting around the kitchen table, having dinner.

Linda looked to Octavia for help.

"It stands for sexually transmitted disease," Octavia said. "You get it from having sex with people you're not married to. So don't have sex until you get married, and when you do get married, don't have sex with anyone except your loyal, faithful, long-suffering, beautiful wife."

Jarrod looked sufficiently alarmed.

Linda gave her a withering look.

"What?" Octavia demanded. "The kid's got to know this stuff sometime."

"He's *nine*. We'll talk about it later," Linda promised Jarrod. "As I was saying, I've color-coded all the residents we talked to and drew lines to people they, um—visited, in loose chronological order, starting in January."

Octavia squinted. "Impressive...but the individual trees don't touch."

"Right." Above the four trees, Linda drew a question mark. "Which means there's someone up here who visited this woman." She drew a line from the question mark to the name at the top of the first tree. "And this woman." She continued drawing lines. "And this woman...and this man."

Octavia's eyebrows went up. "The person we're looking for is bisexual?"

"What's that?" Jarrod asked.

Octavia opened her mouth, but Linda cut in. "Don't even."

She looked at her nephew. "When you're ready for your sex talk, come to me."

"Will you still be here?" he asked, dragging a crinkle fry through ketchup before consuming it in one bite.

Her mistake—the offer had simply popped out. Of course she wouldn't be there when he needed his sex talk, a good year away. "I'll be only a phone call away." She looked back to the diagram. "So we're looking for someone, probably a man, who fu—" She caught herself. "—*visited* Diane F., Barbara A., Anita W., and John C. prior to January."

"Right. But we don't have any other names...you would think at least one of them would've mentioned someone that we'd be able to connect to someone else."

Octavia chewed, her mind churning. "Unless it's a relationship they're each trying to keep secret."

Linda nodded. "Someone they wouldn't have talked about as dating material when we questioned them in the context of the matchmaking service."

"Yet someone they all knew."

"A doctor?"

"Or an employee," Octavia said. The women looked at each other.

"Tyson," they said in unison.

Octavia laughed. "The little tramp. He's got a thing for geriatrics."

"Well, it fits...but we don't know for sure. I'd hate to submit his name to the owner and it not be correct."

Octavia pulled up a browser on her phone. "Let me check a couple of things." She punched in a search string, isolating social media sites. "Bingo.

Tyson Gilly posted that he began his new job at Pleasure Ridge Retirement Home in December."

Linda grinned. "You did it."

Octavia grinned back. "We did it. Again."

"I think this calls for a little celebration—milk and cookies all around!"

The kids cheered and Linda climbed up to remove a bag of chocolate chip cookies from the treat stash, then poured four tall glasses of milk.

Jarrod pulled out a sleeve of cookies and walked around the table, passing out two for each of them. She marveled at the restraint the children showed—at their age, she would've eaten the entire package.

They dunked and ate their cookies together and although Octavia had eaten at some of the finest restaurants in the world, she honestly couldn't remember a better meal. It was...nice.

"This is good, Mommy," Maggie said. "But not as good at Aunt Tavey's pancakes."

Linda raised an eyebrow. "When did Aunt Tavey make you pancakes?"

"After the bad man grabbed her and Jarrod and me saved her life."

Octavia closed her eyes. When she opened them, Linda was looking at her. "What?"

"We promised not to tell," Jarrod muttered to Maggie.

Linda looked from face to face, then back to her. "What are they talking about?"

She drew in a deep breath, then exhaled. "Saturday morning I was out in the yard and a car drove up. A man got out and asked me if I know where Richard is."

"He grabbed Aunt Tavey by the arm," Jarrod said.

"But Jarrod threw a ball and hit him right in the face!" Maggie supplied, with a punch to the air.

"And Max tried to bite his leg," Jarrod said.

"And I threw glitter all over him," Maggie said, grinning.

Linda, however, was not grinning. "Kids, why don't you take your cookies to your room and get started on your homework."

"I don't have any homework," Maggie said. "I'm in the first grade."

"Then go play. I need to talk to Aunt Tavey."

When the children had left the room, Linda nailed her with a glare. "What the hell happened?"

She held up her hands. "I told you—a strange man came up to me and demanded to know where Richard is. I told him I didn't know. Then the munchkin brigade attacked and he left." She smiled a little smile. "That guy is never going to get rid of all that glitter. It will have to grow off."

Linda was not amused. "Did he hurt you? Did he—" She choked back a sob. "Did he touch the kids?"

"No. He grabbed my arm, but he let me go. He didn't touch the kids, and he didn't come into the house."

"And you didn't think this was something I should know?"

"I wanted to spare you the worry."

"This is *my* house, Octavia—I make those decisions." Her green eyes glistened with angry tears.

She nodded, feeling contrite. "You're right...I should've told you."

Linda pushed to her feet and reached for the phone, her body language jerky.

"What are you doing?"

"What you should've done—I'm calling the police."

Which wasn't the full truth, Octavia realized when fifteen minutes later, Detective Oakley Hall arrived and grilled her like a piece of rare meat.

"I've never seen the man before, and I didn't recognize the car." She described the guy and the sedan as best as she could remember, and recited the partial Jefferson County license plate number. He took notes studiously, but his gaze kept straying to Linda, who hugged her arms to her waist and looked paler every passing minute.

"He didn't tell you how he knew your husband?"

"No."

"Or why he wanted to find him?"

"No."

"And *do* you know where your husband is?"

"No."

He closed the notebook. "I'll have the partial plate run to see if I get a hit. Otherwise, call me if you see the car or the guy in the neighborhood." He gave Octavia his card, then turned to Linda. "Can I have a word?"

She nodded, then walked him to the door. Their voices were low, but Octavia could hear the concern in his voice, then lots of silence, which she assumed was moody eye contact.

The man was crushing on Linda, even if she didn't want to see it. But her sister was so noble, she'd probably never act on any feelings between them. Linda was the queen of self-sacrifice.

When Linda came back, Octavia waited for the other shoe to drop.

"How dare you?" Linda was shaking. "How dare you put my children in danger, and not tell me? And worse—make *them* promise not to tell me?"

"They didn't get hurt, sis."

"But they could've! You always miss the point, Susan—always!"

Octavia gritted her teeth. "Don't call me that name."

"Why not? It was your name for thirteen years. You can't just change who you are because you change your name!"

She lifted her chin. "Yes, you can."

Linda's laugh was harsh. "You're still the same selfish person you always were. But I'm not going to let you put my family in danger."

Octavia felt as if she'd been slapped. "Get off your high horse, Linda— you're not mother of the year. Your son hasn't even cried since his father died, for God's sake. And look at this disaster of a house! You're no better mother than our mother was."

As soon as the words were out, she knew she'd gone too far.

Linda's face blanched, and she covered her mouth with her hand.

"I don't know why I said that," Octavia said quietly, shaking her head. "I didn't mean it." She pulled her hand down her face. "I'll leave if you want me to." Inside, though, she was terrified. If Linda said yes, where would she go?

Linda stared at her with big, hollow eyes, and suddenly looked so weary. Finally she heaved a long, shuddering breath. "Go to bed, Octavia."

Then she turned around and shuffled toward the bedroom.

Octavia wanted to run after her, but anger kept her rooted to the spot. Anger at their runaway mother, their criminal father, Linda's irresponsible husband, and Richard on the lam. It was as if the universe had conspired against her and Linda their entire lives to keep them from having a normal sister to sister relationship.

And it didn't look to be improving any time soon.

CHAPTER NINETEEN

LINDA LIFTED HER arms overhead and yawned, stretching as high as she could in the driver's seat of the van. Across the road, thirty-five-year-old Marianne Reynolds had spent most of the past two hours dozing in her backyard on a lawn chair—not exactly the kind of activity that violated her worker's compensation claim that her neck had been fractured and suffered irreparable damage in a worksite fall. In fact, her neck brace seemed to be holding her head at just the right height so she could sleep without her head lolling about and waking her needlessly.

Linda fought another yawn and turned up the radio to help her focus. She glanced over to the empty passenger seat and conceded that a stakeout wasn't as interesting without Octavia along as a sidekick.

Last night's incident came back to her and she groaned in frustration. Sisters knew how to hurt each other, and she and Octavia were better at it than most. Octavia was wrong not to tell her about the stranger coming to her house, but she knew Octavia wouldn't knowingly jeopardize the children.

And in the light of day, she had to admit her sister had hit on some valid points about Linda's parenting skills. She hadn't said anything that Linda herself hadn't thought many times.

She wondered how Octavia was making out in the convenience store today. Her assignment was to spend the day doing janitorial work around the store while keeping an eye on the employees who stocked inventory and ran the cash registers to see if any of them stole.

Linda smiled at the thought of Octavia wielding a mop—her sister simply wasn't cut out for manual labor. So she knew what a personal sacrifice it was for her to try to close out this case for Sullivan's agency. Octavia had never been a fan of Sullivan's—and vice versa—so she was doing this mostly for her.

And her cut of the proceeds, of course.

She put the binoculars up to her face to confirm Ms. Reynolds was still asleep, then she pulled out a crossword puzzle book to keep her mind and hands busy. An hour and three puzzles later, she stretched again and was ready to call it a day—and a bust. The woman must have neck issues—who sat around wearing a neck brace simply to hold their head up?

But just as she was ready to start up the engine, the woman was overrun by four children spilling out the door into the yard with her. She sat in her chair stiffly and accepted kisses from the kids, then watched them play for a while, dozing on and off. One of the children in particular kept coming back to her and climbing on her lap and pulling on her. Even at this distance, Linda could tell the woman was losing patience.

Then she lifted her hands and removed the neck brace. And swung the little girl up to give her a piggy back ride.

Linda's eyes popped wide open. That couldn't be good for a fractured neck. She lifted the camera and took several shots of the exuberant, jostling piggy back ride, and the ones that followed since all the other kids clamored for their own rollicking ride.

Poor Ms. Reynolds—she was a good mother, but a bad employee. It was the classic push-pull of motherhood—if you were a good mother, you were probably bad at something else.

But when was the last time she'd given *her* kids a piggyback ride? She wasn't so sure she was good at anything anymore.

She called Klo at the agency to let her know she'd gotten the pictures the insurance company needed and would email them to her when she got home.

"Has Octavia checked in?" Linda asked.

"No...but I wouldn't expect her to check in with me. You haven't heard from her?"

"No. She's probably busy. By the way, did you ever find that file you were looking for to send to the D.A.?"

"The Foxtrot file? No, I haven't found it, and the A.D.A. is hopping mad about it. I'm afraid in all this housecleaning, I might have shredded it by mistake."

"Well, then it can't be helped, can it?"

"You're right. I'm almost finished cleaning things up in the main part of the office. I was wondering if you'd like for me to go through Sullivan's desk for you and box up his personal things."

It would be easier to let Klo do it...but also a cop out. "Thanks, but I'll do. I'll get to it in a couple days, I promise."

She ended the call and drove home. Weighted down with mail, equipment, and groceries, she practically fell inside, stopped long enough to scratch Max, then turned on the ancient laptop computer in the den. While it booted up, she put away the groceries, then came back to connect the digital camera to send the photos from the worker's comp case to Klo.

Mission accomplished, she started to turn off the computer, then out of idle curiosity, pulled up a search engine and typed in 'Foxtrot.' The results were too numerous to be significant, so she added "Lexington" and "Kentucky" and "crime" to the keywords.

She was halfway down the results page before an entry popped out at her. Foxtrot was the name of the last mount ridden by jockey great Rocky Huff before he was found murdered last fall in Lexington.

A murder that remained unsolved. Was this the "big" case Sullivan had been working on?

She would probably never know. She turned off the machine, calculating she had a little over an hour before the kids got off the school bus. But what to do first?

She went to stand in the opening between the kitchen and the den and turned a full circle—everywhere she looked was a towering to-do pile of supplies and tools for projects that Sullivan had started, but never finished. There had never been a master plan so she wasn't even sure of the intended use of some of the items. If Sullivan found a great deal on something he thought he might need, he brought it home.

She could mow the yard—it certainly needed it.

Or...

She looked in the direction of their bedroom and closed her eyes. *Don't think about it, just do it.*

She made her feet move until she had crossed the threshold of the bedroom. Then she opened the closet and began removing Sullivan's clothes. He was a big man, so his clothes were bulky. The tails and sleeves of his shirts dragged on the floor of the closet where they hung on a low pole. She took them out an armful at a time, then spread them on the bed.

Max lay down next to a pair of Sullivan's shoes and watched.

With her heart in her throat, she removed each item from the hangers to fold, letting the memories wash over her. There were T-shirts from college he still clung to, featuring the names of bars where they'd gone and charity events they'd participated in. There were lots of UK shirts and jackets he'd collected over the years, and countless pairs of the Wrangler jeans he preferred, all in various stages of fading and repair. There was the white shirt with the colorful stains he'd always worn when they took the kids out for ice cream. And the leather jacket she'd bought him for their anniversary three years ago.

His blue police uniform hung under dry cleaner's plastic, where it had remained since he'd left the force. That she would keep.

But not the golf shirts and khakis he'd worn every day to the agency, or his dated sports coats.

There were his many handyman shirts, spotted with paint and solvents.

And sweaters she hadn't gotten around to putting in winter storage.

And exercise clothes he'd bought when he'd gotten the urge last fall to get back into "cop shape," some of which still had the tags on them.

Some of the items she pulled to her face hoping to get a whiff of him, and when she did, the tears rolled down her face.

When his side of the closet was emptied, the different parts of Sullivan's personality were spread across the bed—avid sports fan, policeman, businessman, dad, and husband.

But no more.

Her heart dragging, she gathered cardboard boxes from the garage and folded the clothes neatly before stacking them inside for Goodwill. Some hipster would come across the old "Mickey's Saloon" T-shirt on a one-dollar rack and think it was such a retro find, never giving a thought to the person who'd originally worn it.

"You're getting rid of Dad's things?"

She looked up to see Jarrod standing at the doorway, his face a mask of devastation, his hands fisted at his sides. She moved toward him. "Jarrod, sweetie—"

"You can't! You can't get rid of his stuff!" He began to pummel her with small fists, more flurry than fury. Then he burst into tears and covered his face with his hands.

Her heart broke for him. She gingerly put her arms around his shuddering body, and he allowed her to pull him close as he released two weeks of pent up anger and hurt.

"It's not fair," Jarrod cried against her shoulder.

"I know," she said, rubbing his back. "I feel the same way."

He pulled back, his eyes accusatory. "You haven't even been to visit his grave."

She put her hands around his face. "Yes, I have. But I'll take you and Maggie with me next time."

He nodded, then tried to wipe his face.

"Here, Jarrod," Maggie said from the doorway, holding out a wallowed box of Kleenex. "This is the best thing for crying. They're nice and soft."

Linda bit back a smile as he took a tissue and endured a chubby hug around his waist. She took a tissue for herself and blew her nose, then exhaled.

"I'm giving most of Daddy's clothes to charity...but I thought you might like to keep some of his UK stuff, so I kept this box for you."

Jarrod walked over to the box, mollified.

"What about me?" Maggie asked, all frowns.

She picked up a fedora that Sullivan had worn when he was feeling jaunty and cool, or when Maggie begged him. "I thought you might want Daddy's hat."

"I do!" Maggie exclaimed. "Can I wear it?" She didn't wait for an answer, just plopped in on her head, and was instantly swallowed up in it.

Linda laughed and tipped up the brim to see her daughter's happy blue eyes. Lord, she was Octavia, through and through. "You can wear it anytime you want to. Now...who wants to help me make dinner?"

"Where's Aunt Tavey?" Maggie asked.

"She's working late. She might not be home in time to eat with us."

She wasn't, and the house felt quiet without her. And the call Linda expected to come to pick Octavia up from the convenience store never came. Linda toyed with the idea of calling, but reasoned if she was still working, she wouldn't want to be bothered.

And her sister was a big girl.

"Is Aunt Tavey mad at me for telling about the bad man?" Maggie asked when she tucked her in. "Is that why she didn't come home?"

"No, sweetie, I told you—Aunt Tavey is working."

"She used to be a cheerleader, with pom poms and everything."

"Yes, I know. Go to sleep now."

Linda turned out the light and sighed. She would never be able to impress her little girl the way Octavia did.

She walked back through the house, then stopped when a foreign odor floated to her. *Cigarette smoke.* She followed the scent to the den and noticed the screen door was open to the back deck, which they never used because it was stacked high with replacement lumber. Yet another project.

Fear seized her when she saw the glow of a cigarette. Had the strange man returned looking for Octavia? She picked up Jarrod's baseball bat leaning against the wall, then flipped on the outside light, her heart pounding.

"Jesus," Octavia said, throwing up her hand. "Are you trying to blind me?"

She was sitting in a lawn chair with her feet propped up on the deck railing, still wearing the god-awful striped smock uniform of the convenience store.

Linda stepped outside. "When did you get home?"

Octavia took another drag on the cigarette. "A few minutes ago. The owner of the convenience store offered to drop me off, so I figured I'd save you a trip."

"That was nice of him."

"He had to come by the store anyway to fire the person who was stealing from him—his own son."

"No, really?"

"Pathetic, huh?"

"Well, you know what they say—you can't choose your family."

"Amen to that." She tapped ash.

"How was your day?"

"I smell like nachos, that's how my day was."

"But another case closed."

"Looks like it. How did the surveillance go on the worker's comp case?"

"Bor-ing. But I got the pictures the insurance company needed."

"So we're batting a thousand?"

"Beginner's luck," Linda said.

"Probably." Octavia took another drag, then leaned her head back. "I'm sorry for what I said last night."

Linda scooted a second rickety lawn chair next to Octavia's and dropped into it. "It's okay. I reacted because it's a soft spot of mine—I worry that I'm not a good mother. I mean, what would I know about mothering?"

"You're good with those kids. And they adore you."

Linda pressed her lips together, half afraid to broach the taboo subject on the tip of her tongue. "What do you remember about her?"

Octavia was silent for so long, Linda thought she wasn't going to answer.

"I remember that she loved that sappy Lee Ann Womack song."

"*I Hope You Dance*?"

"That's the one. God, I hate that song. It gives people permission to do stupid things."

Linda waited.

"And I remember the desk you have in your den."

"Yes, that was hers."

"And I remember she didn't have the guts or the decency to say goodbye."

Linda closed her eyes. She remembered that as well. "You've never heard from her?"

"Nope."

"And you don't know where she is?"

"Nope. Nor do I care."

"I lied to Sullivan," Linda said. "I told him our mother was dead. It just seemed...I don't know—easier."

"Don't sweat it—I told Richard the same lie." Octavia gave a harsh laugh. "Jesus, no wonder we're so messed up."

Linda reached over and took the cigarette for a deep drag. She coughed a little, then took another drag and exhaled. "No more secrets, okay?"

"Okay. At least not from each other."

CHAPTER TWENTY

OCTAVIA'S ENTRANCE into the dinner at the Waters-Taub Country Club where she and Richard had been members for as long as they'd been married was everything she'd hoped for.

Voices hushed.

Forks dropped.

The pianist hit a wrong note.

Perfect. And she couldn't have looked more amazing in a pale blue short Versace dress and silver Valentino sandals, if she did say so herself.

"Octavia, how good to see you," Joan Berman said, stepping forward to exchange a fake air-kiss.

"Good to see you, too, Joan."

"No one expected you to be here."

She took two glasses of champagne from the tray of a passing waiter, one for each hand. "Really? Why ever not?"

Joan looked to Katie Lender for help.

"We just didn't know you were back from Lexington," Katie said with a nervous smile. "How is your poor sister doing?"

And she meant "poor" literally. Octavia took a drink from each glass she held, fortified by the tingling bubbles sliding down her throat. "Remarkably well considering the mess her husband left her in." Then she laughed. "That seems to run in the family lately."

"Were you ever able to er...connect with Richard?" Renee Masterson asked delicately.

"No. His phone seems to be dead. Wherever he is, he apparently doesn't have service."

The women exchanged looks.

Octavia rolled her eyes. "Good grief, if you know something, now's the time to tell me. That's why I'm here, you know."

"Well," Renee said, "there are rumors that Richard has gotten mixed up with some unsavory people."

"What kind of people? Who?"

They all shrugged.

"But almost everyone in this room was...approached," Joan said.

"Approached by whom?"

Joan glanced around, as if she was afraid they would be overheard. Indeed, a crowd had gravitated around them, even as everyone avoided making eye contact.

"Spit it out, Joan!"

"Approached by a thug who wanted to know where Richard is."

Octavia felt the blood drain from her face. "A stocky blond guy?"

They all three nodded.

Her mouth tightened. "Which one of you told them where to find *me*?"

Joan and Renee drank from their glasses and slid glances toward Katie. Katie blanched.

Octavia leaned in until they were nose job to nose job. "You led him to my sister's house? He attacked me in front of her *kids*, you mindless twat."

"I—I'm sorry. I didn't know what else to do."

Octavia lifted one of the champagne glasses and tossed it back. The other one, she tossed in Katie's face. She gasped, and so did everyone around them.

Octavia stopped a waiter and traded both empty glasses for full ones. "Where's Patsy?" she asked Joan and Renee. She could always count on Patsy Greenwald to tell her the truth—they had swapped stories about their inattentive husbands in the club sauna more times than she could count.

They were still staring at Katie, who was sputtering. Both of them took a step back.

"What?" she demanded.

"Um, Patsy...seems to be missing, too," Joan said.

"What do you mean, missing too?"

"Her husband hasn't seen her since..."

"Since Richard disappeared," Renee finished, then flinched.

Octavia saw red. Patsy, the woman whom everyone said could be her sister, who groaned when Octavia shared her grievances about Richard's lovemaking.

Octavia emptied another glass of champagne down her throat, tossed the second glass on Katie, dousing her again for good measure, then marched up to the piano.

The pianist saw her coming and stopped playing, his eyes wide. She grabbed the microphone and faced the crowd. "Attention, everyone. As most of you are no doubt aware, my name is Octavia Habersham. Does anybody know where the fuck my husband is?"

The room fell silent and no one moved.

"Okay. Can anyone tell me about the people he's messed up with?" She scanned the room. "Nobody? Okay, well, for those of you who haven't heard, he's been screwing Patsy Greenwald behind my back. Also, we're totally broke and probably can't afford this place anymore, so before I go, I'd like to say something: Every married man in this room who's tried to sleep with me, if you raise your hand right now, I won't call out your name."

Everyone froze. Someone in the back dropped a glass they were holding and it crashed against the floor.

She identified the man and waved. "Yes, Steve Royce, thanks for being honest. I'm sure you and Ailene will have a lot to talk about on the way home. Come on, who else?" She smiled wide. "I've got all night, fellas."

She surveyed the room, her gaze stopping on every man who'd tried to get in her pants over the years until they sheepishly raised their hand. "Don't be shy, Joe Nikko—remember the incident at the Delaneys' Christmas party?" The man's face turned scarlet, but he lifted his fat hand. One by one, hands went up all over the room, including Joan's and Renee's husbands'.

When she was satisfied, she nodded. "I think that about does it for me. Goodnight everyone—enjoy your dinner."

As she walked out, the crowd parted for her. From the looks on their faces, she'd burned a lot of bridges. It struck her that these people had never been her friends—tennis partners, dinner partners, and neighbors—yes. But never friends.

How quickly her life had disintegrated.

She exited the club and waved off the valet, snagging the keys to the van off the board herself. It wasn't hard to find the vehicle since it was the only minivan in the entire parking lot. After tearing out of there, she swung by the house to empty the mailbox and to check if Richard had been there. Her key still worked, so the bank hadn't taken possession...yet.

In Richard's office, she located a phone list for club members and looked up the number for Patsy Greenwald's husband Neil. He answered, but not only did he not know where his wife was, he didn't care. And from the sound of the female laughter in the background, it appeared he'd already moved on.

She ended the call wondering if anything in the world was real or true anymore. Everybody—she and Richard included—seemed to be living disposable lives that could be cast off whenever a person decided to move on, and it didn't matter who got hurt in the process.

Of all those men from the club who'd hit on her, she'd never once been tempted to cheat on Richard. She knew she could be difficult to live with, but she had been faithful.

Her eyes filled with fresh tears. She'd married Richard for a lot of reasons, but she'd picked him over someone like Dunk Duncan because he'd sworn to her he would always be there for her...that he would never leave her.

Like her mother had.

Fooled again.

The house was just as she'd left it. If Richard had been there, she couldn't tell. She went around the house, putting mementos and photo albums in a box, struck by how many of those cherished items were from her childhood and college years and how few were from her marriage.

When she left the house, she drove by Richard's law office, but there was no activity that she could see—and the window was still boarded up from the day she'd thrown a brick through it.

148

As she steered onto the interstate to head back to Lexington, the adrenaline began to ebb and tears threatened as the reality of her situation began to sink in. Two weeks after Richard had disappeared, her pale pink funeral manicure was at the end of its lifespan and she was no closer to finding him, or discovering why he'd left in the first place. The simplest answer was that he and Patsy had run off together, but that didn't explain the thug who was looking for him.

He must be deeply in debt...maybe to a loan shark? Was he hiding out because his life was in danger?

She spotted a bent business card in the console and chewed her lip. She never thought she'd call the man, but she didn't know what else to do.

Octavia used one hand to punch in the number on her phone and listened to it ring two, three times. She was considering hanging up when his voice came on the line.

"Detective Oakley Hall."

CHAPTER TWENTY-ONE

LINDA BLINKED awake slowly, enjoying the soothing suburban sounds of trees swaying, birds chirping, and...

Her eyes flew wide.

Whinnying?

She rolled out of bed and lifted the slat of a mini-blind to look out onto the front yard. Her jaw dropped.

Tied to the trunk of the Bradford pear tree in her yard was a tall, sleek brown horse, happily munching on the clover in her overgrown yard. "What the—?"

Her bedroom door burst open. Jarrod and Maggie were jumping up and down.

"Mommy! Mommy!"

"There's a horse in our yard!"

"So I see."

"How did it get there?" Jarrod asked.

"I have no idea," she murmured. But why did she have the feeling that it had something to do with Octavia coming in last night after they'd all gone to bed?

"Can we go out and pet it?"

"Yeah, can we?"

"No, you may not. You may get dressed and go out on the stoop and wait for me. And don't let Max outside."

They fled.

She pulled on jeans and a top as quickly as she could, then made a beeline for the den. Octavia was sprawled on her back, snoring, wearing a blue satin sleep mask, black camisole and tap pants. All around her were stuffed animals that Maggie was fond of putting in her bed.

Linda leaned over and shook her awake. "Octavia...Octavia, wake up."

She snorted awake and sat up. "What? What's wrong?"

Linda lifted the sleep mask. "There's an animal tied to the tree in my front yard."

Octavia grimaced against the light. "That's a thoroughbred...I thought I taught you something about horses."

Linda tucked her tongue into her cheek. "How did it get there?"

"I brought it home with me last night."

"From where?"

Octavia sighed, already tired of questions. "From Louisville, where I've had it stabled."

"Why did you bring it here?"

"He was about to be repossessed."

Linda squinted. "Horses can be repossessed?"

"I guess so. There was a notice in my mailbox."

Linda was still trying to sort through it all. "You brought it here so the bank can't find it to repossess it?"

"Him. And yes."

"You kidnapped a horse?"

"It's my horse!"

"How on earth did you transport it?"

"Your van did a great job of pulling my horse trailer."

Linda pursed her mouth. "O...kay."

"Mom!" Jarrod yelled from the front door. "Are you coming out?"

"Be right there." She gave Octavia a pointed look. "Coming?"

"If I have to."

"You do."

Octavia groaned, but followed her outside where a nice little crowd of neighbors had gathered to gawk at the splendid animal grazing in their yard. Just as Octavia had said, the minivan sat in the driveway with a horse trailer hitched to it. The horse seemed oblivious to its audience as it picked clean every clump of clover within reach of its long graceful neck.

"Is it yours, Aunt Tavey?" Jarrod asked.

"Yes."

"Can I pet her?"

"Me, too!" Maggie said.

"It's a boy horse. See the—"

Linda stopped her with her arm. "Let's save the anatomy lesson for another time."

Octavia frowned. "Yes, you can pet him if you're very careful. Otherwise, he'll trample you."

Linda's head came around, but Octavia arched an eyebrow. "Kidding, sis. Mercury is as gentle as a lamb."

The kids edged up to him, Maggie, as usual, the braver one who reached out first to touch the horse's neck, her pink mouth open in awe.

"What do you propose we do now?" Linda asked.

Octavia yawned, then gave a little wave. "He'll be fine munching on grass for a couple of days. But at some point I'll have to buy some oats."

Linda stared at her. "You can't be serious."

"What?"

"Octavia, it can't stay here."

"*He*. And why not? Look what an amazing job he's doing on the grass."

The horse lifted its tail and deposited a huge pile of crap on the lawn.

Linda looked at Octavia. "You are so cleaning that up." Then she spotted Nan Boyd marching their way. "Oh, here we go."

"Linda, what is going on here?"

"Just a temporary visitor, Nan. Nothing to worry about."

"This is breaking all kinds of ordinances. *Look* at the flies. Not to mention the safety risk. What if it gets loose and goes on a stampede through the neighborhood? You have kids, you should understand."

"We'll handle it, Nan. Thanks."

"See that you do."

Nan turned and Octavia made a lunge for her, but Linda stopped her. "She's right. You're going to have to find somewhere else to keep him."

A worried look pinched her brow. "I don't have the money right now to pay for boarding him."

Linda pressed her lips together. "I might have a solution."

"What?"

"The guy who owns the pawn shop down from the agency, Grim Hollister?"

Octavia frowned. "What about him?"

"He has a farm and I seem to recall that he has horses. Maybe he'll stable your horse temporarily."

"No way," Octavia said, shaking her head. "I will not be beholden to that base man."

———

Grim Hollister grinned. "What's his name?"

Octavia ground her jaw. "Mercury."

He walked all around the horse, patting him down with long, tapered hands. She noticed with a start that he was wearing the snakeskin boots—but, presumably to cover the ketchup stain, had dyed them bright pink.

And didn't seem to mind one bit.

"What a beauty." Then he looked back at her and winked. "And you have a good-looking horse, too."

"You're hysterical. May I see your stables, please?"

"Sure, right this way." He led Mercury down a path and she followed, taking the opportunity to look around.

The man had a prime piece of land located close to Keeneland race track and Blue Grass Airport...but he'd set on it a hick cabin that looked like it had been made from red Lincoln Logs—ugh. Too rustic for her tastes.

But she supposed it suited him.

He walked ahead of her, lean and long-limbed, dressed in dark jeans and his ever-present black T-shirt. She guessed some women would find him and his body artwork attractive. His ponytail extended past the nape of his neck about three inches. He looked like he worked out, but he probably got those arms from doing something greasy like retooling car engines or buffing out his crotch-rocket motorcycle.

When the horse barn came into view, though, she pursed her mouth.

Not bad.

It was a classic style that resembled a church from the profile, minus the steeple. A center aisle design, she could tell from here, with stalls on both sides and a loft with glass windows along the length of the inset. Painted white, with a red roof. And nicer than the home she'd grown up in.

"Does it pass muster?" Grim asked.

"I'll reserve judgment until I see the inside."

His laugh was low and throaty. "Okay." He tied Mercury off to a white hitching post in front, and opened the double doors.

Inside, the ceilings were high and the lighting, excellent. Ceiling fans moved slowly overhead. Everything was clean and shiny. The floor was concrete and studded with drains. There were five stalls on either side of the center aisle, three of them occupied with horses that apparently were accustomed to Grim, as they hung out their heads and stretched their necks toward him.

"Yours?" she asked, reaching out a hand to scratch the head of a white mare.

"The mare and the big quarter horse are mine. The gelding is a rescue animal."

"So Mercury would be your only boarder?"

"Yep."

"And do you have a helper?"

"Nope."

"Will you have time to care for him properly?"

"Probably. But you're welcome to come out any time to ride." He grinned. "Him, of course."

She narrowed her eyes. "And how much will you charge me for temporary boarding?"

"Linda said you were a little strapped for cash at the moment."

God, she hated being poor! "That's right. So what kind of deal can you cut me?" She angled her head. "And don't even think about some kind of lewd barter."

"No?" He looked disappointed, then nodded to her finger. "I figure that emerald ring will take care of it."

She gasped. "This is my engagement ring! And it's worth a lot more than a few months of horse boarding."

"Really? And how much is it worth not to call your bank and tell them where to find the horse?"

Linda had revealed way too much to this goon. "You wouldn't!"

"Afraid I would. Horse stealing is a crime, you know. A hundred years ago, you would've been hanged."

"Don't be ridiculous. He's my horse....he's just not paid for yet."

"Po-tat-o, po-tot-to." He held out his hand.

She screwed up her mouth, then pulled off her emerald ring and dropped it into his palm "I hate you."

"Things change," he said with a cocky smile, then pocketed the ring.

Ooh! Octavia threw imaginary daggers into his back as he went outside to fetch Mercury.

Of one thing she was certain—she would never *not* hate this man.

CHAPTER TWENTY-TWO

THE FEMALE receptionist at the Lexington Division of Police offered Linda a smile through an opening in a thick glass wall. "May I help you?"

"I'm Linda Smith...the wife of the l-late Sullivan Smith, who used to be on the force."

The woman's smile turned to an expression of sadness. "Yes, I knew your husband, Mrs. Smith. I'm very sorry for your loss."

She inclined her head, then held up a card. "The precinct sent flowers to the service. I was hoping you could post this thank-you note in a public place, maybe in a break room?"

"I'd be happy to."

"Thank you. Also, is Detective Hall available?"

"I'll check." She picked up a phone and punched in a number, then spoke into the receiver before setting it down. "Detective Hall will be right out."

Linda stepped back to wait, nodding at uniformed officers as they passed by. She recalled Jarrod's sentiments that he wished his dad had remained a cop. She understood what her son had meant—being a police officer was a noble calling. Seeing Sullivan in his uniform had never failed to stir her.

Oakley appeared through an open door, his expression tentative. "Hi, there. Is everything okay at home?"

"Yes," she assured him. "Is this a bad time to talk?"

"Never for you. Come on back."

She followed him through a security door and into the buzz of a busy office with an open desk configuration. Phones rang and voices vied to be heard. An announcement was being made over the PA system that no one seemed to be paying attention to.

He led her to a cluttered desk against a wall. "Sorry I can't offer something with more privacy."

"This is fine." His work area was devoid of personal items—no photographs or mementos...that was Oakley. She took the seat he cleared off for her. "I want to talk to you about something."

He lowered himself into his chair. "About Octavia's situation? She called me last night. I think I'm close to having some information for her."

Linda frowned. "Octavia called you?"

He frowned. "That's not why you're here?"

"No. But what's going on?"

He hesitated. "I'm not sure I should– "

"Oakley, she's living in my house. Whatever's going on might affect my kids."

"Right. Well, your sister was at a cocktail party last night and got the impression that her husband might be afraid for his life."

Linda raised an eyebrow. "You mean from Octavia?"

He smiled. "No. From the man who came to your house. I'm still trying to find a plate match to the partial Octavia got. But it got me thinking that if Habersham *was* afraid of something—maybe a client or someone else connected to a case—he might've requested protective custody."

Linda brightened. "You think that's where he's been?"

"I'm waiting for a call back from the Jefferson County D.A.'s office to see if they have any information they can give me."

She felt a surge of affection for him. "Thank you, Oakley."

"Don't thank me yet." He lifted his hands. "So, if you didn't come to talk about Octavia, what did you want to talk about?"

"I wondered if you knew anything about a big case Sullivan was working on, something maybe for the D.A.'s office here in Fayette County?"

He looked confused. "Why do you want to know?"

"The D.A. asked Klo for a case file that she can't find...something about Foxtrot?"

"It makes sense that Sully would be working on something for the D.A.'s office at any given time. Most investigators do."

"So you don't know anything about Foxtrot?"

He shook his head. "I can't say that I do."

She nodded, feeling foolish, not even sure what she'd hoped to gain from talking to Oakley. "Okay...thanks." She pushed to her feet. "I'd better be going."

"So soon?"

She pointed to her lanyard. "Those chips won't stock themselves."

"I'll walk out with you." He led her back through the labyrinth of desks to the door that spilled into the lobby. As they were going out, another man was coming in. He looked vaguely familiar to Linda and when he caught her eye, he did a double-take.

"You're Mrs. Smith, aren't you?"

"Yes, I am."

"Milton Jacobson. I attended your husband's service."

"That was very kind of you."

"I was sorry to hear about Sullivan—unlike a lot of guys around here, I never had a problem with him when he was on the force."

Linda blinked.

"Jacobson, Mrs. Smith is running late," Oakley said.

"Right. Good to see you, ma'am."

She made some appropriate remark. When he was gone, she looked at Oakley. "What was he talking about?"

"Don't pay any attention to him." But she could tell the man's comment had bothered him, too.

She touched his arm. "Oakley, what aren't you telling me?"

He wavered.

"Oakley...please."

He looked aggrieved. "Sully didn't want you to know."

"Know what?"

"That he left the department on bad terms."

She drew back. "I thought he left because he wanted to strike out on his own."

"I'm sure that was part of it...but he also had some enemies in the department."

She was stunned. "Why would Sullivan have enemies?"

"Oh, you know Sully—he had a knack for saying the wrong thing at the wrong time. It made for some bruised egos and bad feelings. It just got to be too tense around here."

"He was asked to leave?"

Oakley drew his hand over his mouth. "The captain thought it would be best."

She inhaled sharply as betrayal stabbed her. How could Sullivan not have told her the truth? And how could Oakley have kept his secret? Humiliation rolled over her that Oakley knew Sullivan had kept her in the dark about the reason for his career change. What must he think of their marriage?

"I have to go," she said.

"Linda, don't hold this against Sully."

"Or you?"

He pressed his lips together, but didn't say whatever was playing through his mind.

"Goodbye, Oakley."

"I'll be in touch about Octavia."

"If you find out something, call *her*," she said pointedly, then turned and left.

Outside she gulped for air, feeling like the rug had been pulled out from under her—again. How dare Sullivan exclude her from information that affected her livelihood. How many other things about her husband did she not know?

As she went about her vending rounds, Linda tried to shake the resentment that had sprung up in her heart toward Sullivan...he was gone now and nothing else should matter.

But it did. It mattered that she'd fashioned her life around his, to be his loving, supportive partner, and in return he'd disrespected her so thoroughly. Sullivan had always been dismissive of her trivia games and puzzles and the prizes she'd won. Patronizing, now that she thought about it. He wouldn't have believed she was capable of tackling the open cases he'd left behind...much less closing them.

While she was stocking the vending machines in the building where she and Octavia had run into Dunk Duncan, she recalled him saying he was there to meet with an assistant D.A. After the last bag of Ruffles had been refilled, she checked the building directory and found the D.A.'s offices. Then she scanned individual names. Klo had mentioned the A.D.A.'s last name in a conversation, but she couldn't remember it.

But she recognized it when she saw it—*Houston*. B.L. Houston, 4th floor.

She took the stairs to the fourth floor, then stuck the box of chips inventory under a draped table in the hallway, and slid the telltale lanyard into a pocket. She found the correct office, then explained to the secretary that she was there to see A.D.A. Houston about the Foxtrot case.

The reaction was impossible to miss. The secretary excused herself, then returned to lead Linda into an office where an attractive black woman was Skyping a meeting while eating a cup of Greek yogurt, obviously her lunch. She held up a finger to indicate she was wrapping up and to have a seat in the chair in front of her desk.

Linda sat nervously, more than a little intimidated by the sheer number of leather-bound tomes on the woman's bookshelves, the framed diplomas on the wall, and the stacks of paper on the work tables. All of it was so much more exciting than her life.

A tone sounded and Linda looked up to see the woman walking toward her, hand extended.

"Hello, I'm A.D.A. Beverly Houston."

"Linda Guy. Er, Smith."

"Nice to meet you, Ms. Guy-Smith. I understand you want to talk about Foxtrot?"

"My late husband Sullivan Smith was a private investigator, and it's my understanding he was working on the Foxtrot case for you."

Her gaze flicked over Linda's capri pants, T-shirt, and Keds sneakers. "No offense, but what does that have to do with you?"

"I took over his open cases, and I thought I might be of assistance on this case as well. It does concern the murder of jockey Rocky Huff, yes?"

As soon as the awkward pause was underway, she regretted saying any-thing...regretted coming here...regretted getting out of bed this morning.

The woman clasped her manicured hands in front of her. "Are you an investigator, Mrs. Smith?"

And just like that, she'd lost the courtesy of the hyphenated last name. "No. But I've been able to close Sullivan's other cases—"

"I'm sorry to interrupt you, but I'm very busy, and you're in way over your head here. The D.A.'s office works only with professional investigators. And to be frank, I only gave this assignment to Mr. Smith as a favor to Detective Hall, who said his friend needed the work."

Linda's cheeks flamed.

A.D.A. Houston picked up a notebook and scanned what was written there. "According to my records, we're waiting for Mr. Smith's case notes to be sent to our office."

"Yes, we're working on that now."

"Very good, we'll expect to receive them at your earliest convenience." The woman extended her hand for another shake, this one a clear dismissal. "And I'm very sorry for your loss."

"Yes," Linda said, pushing to her feet.

By the time she'd walked to the door, A.D.A. Houston was already on the phone, taking another meeting. Linda slunk out, tingling with humiliation, then backtracked to the hallway and slid the ugly vending lanyard over her head.

"This is your job now," she murmured to herself.

But the box of inventory wasn't under the table—someone had swiped it.

Great—there went her profits for the day.

The irony of getting ripped off outside the D.A.'s office wasn't lost on her. In a way, though, it seemed fitting.

It was a good reminder of her role in the overall scheme of things.

CHAPTER TWENTY-THREE

OCTAVIA SPREAD HER mail on the kitchen table, dread churning in her stomach. When had little sealed envelopes become such a source of anxiety?

When the news they contained had become so unwelcome: Past due bills, lien notices, and offers to help facilitate bankruptcy, no doubt triggered by her recent credit tumble.

Her phone rang, sending her pulse higher. As always, she hoped it was Richard, but the name on the ID screen was Detective Oakley Hall.

She connected the call. "This is Octavia." Linda walked into the kitchen for a coffee refill.

"Hello, Detective Hall calling."

"Yes, Detective Hall, do you have news for me?"

Standing at the coffeemaker with her back to the table, Linda's head turned.

"I do...but it's not quite what I expected."

She could tell from the tone of his voice it wasn't good news. She steeled herself. "I'm listening."

"A representative of the Jefferson County D.A.'s office called me this morning. They're familiar with Richard Habersham, all right, but he hasn't been taken into protective custody. They're issuing a warrant for his arrest."

She couldn't pull air into her lungs. "What...for?"

"Conspiracy to commit murder."

"Murder?" It was so absurd, Octavia actually relaxed. "That's insane."

Linda turned around, her eyes wide.

"The story is a little murky, but Habersham is accused of leaking confidential information about one of his clients that resulted in the man being stabbed to death."

She closed her eyes. If Richard had done what they were accusing him of, his life was over. A few weeks ago she would've said her husband was incapable of that kind of treachery...but now she really didn't know.

"And I take it Richard knew a warrant was imminent?"

"Yes."

She pushed her hand into her hair. "So he's a fugitive?"

"He will be by noon today unless he turns himself in. There's a bolo on his car, and the Greenwald woman's, too. She could be charged with aiding and abetting."

Small comfort for Patsy's betrayal.

"I'll call you if I hear anything else."

"Okay...thanks." She disconnected the call, then looked at Linda and shook her head.

"What's going on?"

She relayed the news, still in shock.

"You had no idea?"

"None." She gave a little laugh. "You think you know someone."

Linda nodded. "I know what you mean."

Jarrod yelled for Linda to come and help him with something in his room. She pushed away from the counter and squeezed Octavia's shoulder when she walked by. "Oakley is right—the police will find him."

But when? She felt as if her entire life was on hold until Richard reappeared. *That's what you get for molding your life around someone else.*

Her mind whirled in all directions. A stack of folded *Louisville Courier-Journal* newspapers sat on the end of the table, mocking her. Richard's arrest would just be something else their friends and neighbors could read about in the papers, along with their home foreclosure and most likely, forthcoming bankruptcy.

The picture of a college beauty queen on the front page caught her eye. She unfolded the paper and stared at the pretty woman's Vaseline smile and tiny waist nipped in under her evening gown by Ace bandages. Those were the days, she thought with longing, when she had a crown on her head and the world at her feet.

Now she was sitting at a grubby table nursing a headache with a hound lying on her feet.

She became engrossed in the story of the young coed who had survived flesh-eating bacteria and started a foundation to refurbish prosthetics for the poor. She was impressed at the woman's ingenuity. In the theater of pageantry, surviving a disease and doing something for the poor was an almost unbeatable combination. The only reason she'd beat out that do-gooder epileptic Deena Freeman for Miss Kentucky was because the woman had a wardrobe malfunction during her dance routine that had offended the conservative judges.

Darn, if only someone hadn't stolen the double-sided tape from Deena's toiletry bag.

Octavia turned to the back of the paper to read the rest of the story, scanning for judges' names she recognized, and finding a few. She nibbled at her thumbnail. It was looking more and more as if she were going to have to get a job, dammit, at least in the interim. Maybe she should get back into pageanting.

She started to close the newspaper when a name in another section jumped out at her: Carla Buczkowski....her maid.

Police were called to a home on Ocala Avenue where they found the body of Carla Buczkowski, dead of a gunshot wound in an apparent home invasion. The police have no suspects.

She gasped into her hand—Carla, dead? How senseless. She couldn't imagine what the woman would've had that was worth killing her over, but people would steal anything these days. She was furious and hurt at the thought that she and Richard might've been having an affair, but she hadn't wanted her dead.

Although the voicemail message she'd left the day she'd called Carla from the Waffle House hadn't been exactly friendly.

Octavia checked the date of the article, then checked her phone for outgoing calls. Her throat constricted. Carla's body had been found the day she'd called her.

Had the woman been lying on the floor dying, while her phone rang and Octavia ranted to her voicemail?

When she reread the brief piece, a memory stirred. Ocala Avenue...where had she seen that street name recently?

Then it hit her—on Richard's background report, one of the parking tickets he'd received was on Ocala Avenue. So he had been to Carla's home.

And Richard had bought a handgun.

But that made no sense—why would Richard kill Carla? What did she have that—?

The evidence envelope.

Had Carla been killed because of it—by Richard or by someone else?

And if so, before she died, had she revealed that she'd given it to Octavia?

Her mind reeled, but she calmed herself enough to remember that the thug had shown up at Linda's house *after* Carla had been killed—if he'd had anything to do with Carla's death and if she'd told him Octavia had the envelope, he wouldn't have let a glitter storm stop him.

Which took her back to Richard. But if Richard had killed Carla, and if Carla had told him she'd given the envelope to her, Richard knew where to find her...and he hadn't shown up.

So either Carla's death had nothing to do with the envelope...or she hadn't revealed that she'd given it to Octavia.

And besides, Richard was obviously a lot of things—a liar and a bad money manager and a terrible lover and yes, probably a whoremonger—but he wasn't a killer.

She didn't think.

Still...she needed to take precautions with the envelope until he could be located.

If she went to the police with what she knew, she would incriminate Richard in another murder.

But neither did she want to leave the envelope in Linda's house.

An unpleasant alternative came to mind. She made a face, but went to the den to unearth the purse where the padded envelope was mixed in with miscellaneous old mail.

"Sis," she called, "mind if I borrow the van for a quick errand?"

"No, go ahead."

She drove to the strip mall and wedged the van into the packed parking lot. Apparently Saturdays were busy for all the businesses, except for the investigation agency. She shook her head at the pathetic little sign and the dark windows. Sullivan might've been good at his job, but the man had no salesmanship.

The pawn shop, no surprise, was hopping with people looking to unload some piece of garbage and pick up a different piece of garbage to take home. Grim was helping a customer near the back counter where, she remembered, he kept the "good stuff."

She sidled her way through the crowd trying not to touch anyone. When she approached the counter, she scanned the jewelry display, expecting to see her beloved emerald ring. The fact that she didn't see it only disheartened her more—he'd probably already sold it.

Grim noticed her and excused himself from a customer, then walked over. "This is a nice surprise."

She swallowed a retort, mindful of her chore. "I need a favor."

His black eyebrows rose a fraction. "Okay. Name it."

She pulled the envelope out of her bag. "I need you to store this for me somewhere safe, no questions asked."

"What's in it for me?"

"Absolutely nothing."

He studied her for a few seconds, then held out his hand, palm up. "Okay."

She put the envelope in his hand, then forced out the words, "Thank you."

"You're wel—"

But she was already threading her way back through the crowd. When she left the seedy little store, however, Octavia conceded the impossible had just happened.

She hated him a little less.

CHAPTER TWENTY-FOUR

KLO GAVE LINDA a sad smile. "I left everything in Sullivan's office the way it was, just tidied a bit when I looked for the missing file."

"You still haven't found it?"

"No. At this point, I'm thinking it's lost. Or maybe Sullivan had already sent it to the D.A.'s office and it got misplaced over there."

"Maybe," Linda agreed.

"Anyway, yell if you need me."

Linda nodded toward Octavia who had parked herself behind a desktop computer, then lowered her voice. "You sure you don't mind my sister being here?"

"I don't mind. But if I knew what she was doing, I might be able to help."

"I'll let you know if I want your help," Octavia said without looking up.

Klo straightened, then huffed back to her own corner.

Looking heavenward, Linda put her hand on the doorknob and took a deep breath.

She pushed open the door and experienced an immediate sense of loss. The small office seemed to be in motion—books lay open on Sullivan's oak desk and the chair was scooted back, as if Sullivan had left in a hurry.

Which he had, she acknowledged, with a fresh, deep pang.

The leased desktop computer was sitting with cords wrapped around it, waiting to be picked up at month-end, only a week away. Then the agency would be closed for good.

Klo had stacked empty cardboard boxes in the corner for her to use. She started at the bookshelf, pulling framed family photographs of the children at various ages, and one of Sullivan's parents.

She'd gotten a card from his mother Marbella, with apologies and excuses for not attending her son's funeral, and a check inside for twenty-five dollars with strict instructions that it be used "for the children."

Her children were being deprived of grandparents from both sides. She'd promised herself, though, that when the children were out of school for the summer, she would arrange for them to visit with their paternal grand-mother somehow.

It wasn't as if their maternal grandparents were going to be available any-time soon.

She picked a few autographed novels from the shelf to add to the box. Most of the materials were industry related—his multitude of manuals from the police academy, and from the coursework he'd taken to become a reg-istered private investigator. There were volumes on weapons, crime scene investigation, Kentucky statutes and constitutional law. Sullivan had prided himself on being a good investigator, and his book collection backed up the fact that he was thorough. But she suspected his quiet and sometimes morose personality kept him from attracting as much new business as he needed to truly thrive.

Still, his library was impressive and was probably valuable to someone. She made a mental note to tell Octavia to call Dunk Duncan to see if he wanted it—as far as she was concerned, he could have the books for the cost of hauling them away. She'd rather they be put to good use.

She walked around his desk and stopped to stare at the floor. A sob welled in her chest. This was where Stone had found him, collapsed. It was agonizing to think of how long he'd lain there, helpless. A small dark stain on the carpet could've been anything—or there for years—but it struck her as ominous. She had to look away.

The best part of the office was the window behind the desk, but someone had pulled the curtain closed. She pushed it back to allow natural light to flow into the room.

That was better.

A picture of her and Sullivan sat on the window ledge. Her heart crowded her throat as she picked it up and blew off the dust. They had both been in college—it had been taken early in their relationship. She removed the back from the frame and unfolded the picture.

Oakley Hall sat on the other side of her, leaning in.

She refolded the picture and put it back in the frame, then added it to the box.

A half-empty cup of coffee sat on the window ledge, and the sight of it was heartbreaking—another interrupted routine task. Next to the window, a ficus tree was drooping. She poured the stale coffee into the root ball. No use for anything else to die around here.

At last, she turned to Sullivan's desk and began to empty it. It was a big, clubby model without a lot of usable drawer space. The contents were mostly toiletries he kept on hand, a few magazines, and a couple of books. The first book brought new tears to her eyes. *How to Tie Knots*. The frayed length of white rope inside the book was proof of why he hadn't yet taught Jarrod how to tie knots for Scouts—he was still practicing himself.

The second book caused an uptick in her pulse: *The Life of a Thoroughbred Jockey*. Part how-to, part memoir, the book contained biographies and interviews with some of the industry's most celebrated jockeys. She put the book on the desk and let it fall open naturally...and it opened to the page on Rocky Huff.

That couldn't be a coincidence.

A knock at the door sounded. She looked up to see Octavia. "Trouble." She opened the door wider to reveal Jarrod standing in the reception area, his head hanging. Oakley stood behind him.

She came out of the office and noticed Jarrod's shirt was torn and stained with—*blood*? "What on earth?"

When Jarrod looked up, he was sporting a shiner. She gasped and sank to the floor in front of him. "What happened?"

"I got in a fight at school," he mumbled.

She frowned and lifted his jaw so she could get a better look at his eye. "You know better than that. What happened?"

He shrugged. "I don't know...Evan Padgett said something and I just got mad and I punched him in the nose." He pointed to his shirt. "That's his blood."

"I thought you and Evan were friends."

"We are," he said miserably.

"What did he say to make you mad?"

"I don't even remember." He started to cry, but she shushed him with a hug.

"Why don't Klo and I take you to Waffle House and get you a T-shirt?" Octavia asked.

He looked at Linda and she nodded. Then she gave the women a grateful look.

When they left, she looked at Oakley. She hadn't gotten over their last conversation. "How did you get involved?"

"Jarrod called me. I went to pick him up from school."

"The school released him to you?"

"Only because I'm a police officer and his godfather."

"Did they say anything about what happened?"

He handed her a piece of paper. It was from the school counselor. She suggested that Jarrod had rage issues connected to the loss of his father, and she recommended grief counseling.

Linda refolded the letter, feeling like a total failure. "I'm falling down on my job, it seems. I need to be paying more attention to my children."

"No one thinks you're falling down on your job. This hasn't been easy for anyone, but for you, most of all. It's going to take time."

She nodded. "I know."

"I'm here for you...and for the kids."

"I appreciate that, Oakley, I really do. But we'll be just fine."

He shifted foot to foot. "I got a phone call from A.D.A. Beverly Houston."

A flush began to work its way up her neck. "Oh."

He gave a little laugh. "She said you came to see her, that you'd taken over Sullivan's cases?"

Her chin went up. "That's right. Octavia and I took on the open cases... and we closed them." She faltered. "Well...except for Foxtrot...which by the way, you lied to me about. You said Sullivan wasn't working on it and A.D.A. Houston said she gave him the job on your referral."

"I said I couldn't *say* if he was working on it."

"That's not fair."

He put his hands on his hips. "Why are we even talking about this? You were way out of line to go see the A.D.A. about a confidential case that you're not a part of."

"I just happened to be in the building and stopped by to ask a couple of questions about a file that we can't seem to find."

"Just happened to be in the building?" Then realization dawned. "You just happened to be in the building stocking potato chips and thought you'd drop in to chat with the A.D.A.?"

"You act like investigative work is some kind of closed club."

His eyes bulged. "It is! It's for law enforcement professionals. You're a stay-at-home mom!"

She stopped. He was right...so why did it feel like such a putdown?

"Duly noted," she said quietly.

"Linda—"

She saw the trio returning with Jarrod sporting a brand new Waffle House T-shirt. "Thank you very much for coming to Jarrod's assistance today...and mine. Goodbye, Oakley."

"Are you leaving, Uncle Oakley?" Jarrod asked.

"Yeah. See you soon, champ. No fighting, okay?"

"Okay."

Linda hugged Jarrod to her and over his head, watched Oakley stride to his unmarked sedan and climb inside.

She could hear his car door slam from there.

CHAPTER TWENTY-FIVE

"WELCOME TO Waffle House," Brittany said. "Coffee, half and half, right?"

Octavia looked up. "Yes." Under the bill cap, the girl actually had really nice bone structure.

"Do I have something on my face?"

"No, and that's the problem. You know, if you wore just a little mascara, your eyes would really pop."

The girl frowned. "I don't have the time to fool with all that crap."

Octavia read between the lines. *I can't afford makeup and wouldn't know what to buy if I did.*

"Do you want to order something to eat?"

"I'll have that chicken salad thing again."

"Good choice. Coming right up."

Octavia massaged her temples to ward off the building explosion in her head, then decided a cigarette would calm her nerves more. She and Klo had been working for the better part of three days to piece together Richard's activities for the past few months to try to predict where he might be hiding out.

So far, nothing had panned out. Klo had good connections with the Lexington Police Division because, no big surprise, she used to be a stripper. And she must've been a good one, because every time she called with a question, it got answered.

She pulled out a cigarette and lit it with a two-dollar lighter.

If Richard were indeed hiding out. Lately she'd started to worry he might be dead. What if that thug had found him?

She drew on the cigarette, then exhaled.

She certainly hoped not...because she wanted first crack at him.

The only thing she hadn't shared with Klo or the police was the evidence envelope she had. She didn't know what move to make, and the stress was killing her. If she turned it in, it might mean worse things for Richard, and as furious with him as she was, she wasn't ready to send him up the river yet...not while her boat was still attached to his.

She took another drag, then exhaled.

The worst thing was knowing this could go on and on—they didn't even know if Richard was still in the area. He could be any-fucking-where.

A man's cough sounded, then Grim swung into the booth opposite her. "I hate to break it to you, but you can't smoke in here."

She frowned. "Why the hell not?"

"Because those things will kill you."

"Really?" She thumped the menu. "And sausage gravy and biscuits, with an order of smothered hash browns won't?"

"You've got a point. But death by biscuit generally takes longer. And there's no such thing as second-hand cholesterol." He reached over and removed the cigarette from her fingers and snubbed it out on a saucer. "What's got your La Perlas in a twist?"

"How do you know what brand of underwear I have on?"

"Lucky guess for a lady who refuses to buy jewelry in a pawn shop."

"Well, if you must know," she said, counting on her fingers, "in the last three weeks, my husband left me stranded, then I found out we're broke, then I found out he's having an affair, then I found out he's a fugitive for conspiracy to commit murder."

He pursed his mouth. "That actually explains a lot. But any man who would have an affair on you needs to be locked up anyway."

"Don't try to cheer me up."

He held up his hands. "I wouldn't dare." Then he leaned in. "So...that thing I'm keeping for you...does it have anything to do with...anything?"

"I don't know what's inside. It's an evidence envelope, so if I break the seal, then whatever's in it will be compromised."

"So would it help if you could tell what's inside?"

She arched an eyebrow. "Can you do that?"

"If whatever is inside is solid. I have at least a couple of handheld x-ray devices in the shop. Depends on how good the resolution is, but we should be able to get some idea."

She was already on her feet and heading toward the door.

Grim lifted his hands. "Can I have lunch?"

"Afterward."

"Me and my big mouth."

Inside the pawn shop, Grim led her to a room in the rear where he produced the envelope and a handheld x-ray machine. But it took them a while to figure out exactly how to use it.

"This isn't working," she said.

"Patience," he chided, and hit the reset button again to allow the machine to reboot.

She sat back in her chair with a heavy sigh.

"By the way, Ms. Would Never Buy Anything From a Pawnshop, guess what came in earlier this week?"

"I'm not guessing."

"A Picasso."

She laughed. "Right."

"I'm not kidding. This couple had a Picasso drawing and a, a—" He snapped his fingers. "The art glass guy, what's his name?"

She sat forward. "Chihuly?"

"Yeah, a Chihuly bowl. Should've known you'd know the name."

Her heart galloped in her chest. "Did you buy them?"

"No way—I don't keep that kind of cash lying around. I told them they'd have to find a gallery or a museum."

"Do you think they did?"

"Maybe, but they made me nervous...I kind of got the feeling the items were stolen."

"They were—*from my house.*"

His eyes widened. "No kidding?"

"Dark-haired slender man? And did the woman look like me?"

"That's the guy...and the woman had dark hair, but she looked nothing like you."

Okay, that scored him a few points. "You're going to have to talk to the police. But you can't mention this envelope."

He looked wary. "Okay." Then he held up the x-ray. "Let's try this again." This time he was able to get a passable image of the contents of the envelope on the machine screen.

But to Octavia it looked like a flat textured blob.

"What is it?"

He turned the image right, then left. "It's a bullet."

"It doesn't look like a bullet."

"It a bullet that's already been shot." He looked at her, his expression grave. "And if it's evidence, then that probably means it killed someone."

CHAPTER TWENTY-SIX

"...SO IF ANYTHING becomes available, please keep me in mind," Linda said. "Thank you, Samantha."

She ended the call, crossed off Samantha's name, then went to the next person on the list she'd made of friends, neighbors, and mere acquaintances who might be able to recommend her for a job that would dovetail into a career. Maybe something clerical or administrative. Preferably something with benefits.

She dialed the next number and forced cheer into her voice. "Hi, Jill, this is Linda Guy Smith."

"Hi, Linda. I didn't know 'Guy' was your middle name."

"It's my maiden name."

"Oh. How *are* you?"

She was finding it hard to strike a balance between sounding well enough to be a competent employee, but pitiful enough for people to want to help her. "Fine...you know—most days."

"Depression, huh?"

"Well—"

"Of course you're depressed. Who wouldn't be, losing your husband like that, and you still a young, vibrant woman?"

She took the opening. "I'm glad you think so, Jill. Actually, I called because I'm putting out feelers to get back on a career track."

"Oh? What did you do before you were a stay-at-home mom?"

"I was a young mother, so I didn't get a chance to work outside the home much."

"I was a young mother, too, but I also had a career." Her voice vibrated with censure.

"I really admire that, Jill. You're way ahead of me. I guess I'm a late-bloomer."

"Well...what is your degree in?"

"Actually, I didn't get a chance to finish my college degree. But I studied political science at UK for two years."

"Oh. Well, Linda, in this day and age, I'm sure you realize that getting a job without a college education and no work experience is going to be very difficult."

She closed her eyes. "Yes, I do. That's why I'm reaching out to friends like you who might be able to recommend me because of my character...and my circumstances."

She'd gotten to the point where she actually counted the length of the awkward pauses to see who could hold out the longest. *One Mississippi....two Mississippi...three Mississippi—*

"Absolutely, I will keep you in mind the next time I hear of an opening you'd be qualified for."

Milly Washburn still held the record at seven Mississippi's.

"Thank you very much," Linda said. "Meanwhile, can I email you a resume and a cover letter?"

"Sure. You take care, Linda."

The line went dead before Linda could ask for her email address.

"Perfect," she murmured.

All morning she'd spoken to people who felt sorry for her, but didn't hold out much hope of her finding a job considering the education and career decisions she'd made.

Meaning, she'd done everything wrong.

She looked at the last remaining name on the list and sighed. *Oakley.*

She inhaled and swallowed her pride in one gulp, then dialed his number.

He answered on the second ring. "Hi, there. I didn't expect to hear from you."

"Well, the other day you said you were there for me."

"Of course I am."

She gave a little laugh. "I'm calling in a chit."

"Whatever you need, I'm your man."

She bit down on her tongue. That was the last thing she needed to hear. "You know the vending machine job isn't exactly a career builder, so I was wondering if you know of anyone who has a job opening I might be qualified for."

"Actually, I might. But it's a nine-to-five job, and would be a conflict with the kids' schedules, especially in the summer."

"We'll make it work," she said, sounding more sure than she felt.

"Let me make a phone call, and I'll get back to you."

"Okay...thank you."

"Sure thing."

She ended the call, feeling a tad better. Even if the job didn't materialize, at least it had broken the ice between them. Oakley had always been one person she couldn't stand knowing things weren't good between them.

A whirring noise in the front yard caught her attention. She hoped it wasn't another surprise guest from Octavia, but she doubted it since her sister had been spending the days at the agency with Klo trying to figure out where Richard might be. They were an unlikely pair, but apparently had reached some kind of alliance to use the final week of the agency's resources to try to find a fugitive.

She stepped to the window and looked outside to see Stone Calvert pushing a lawn mower across her neglected yard. She smiled in surprise. Klo must've sent him over, bless them both.

She went to the fridge and poured two glasses of lemonade, ready to take a break herself. On the way to the front door, she stopped at the mirror to survey her appearance. Good...but not great. She finger-combed her hair and gave her cheeks a pinch, then was irritated with herself. What did it matter? Stone had seen her a hundred times.

Although she wouldn't mind dispelling the picture of her having a meltdown in the parking lot of the funeral home.

She opened the door and walked outside, lifting the glasses to get his attention. He looked up and waved, then turned off the lawnmower. "I didn't know if you were home." He pulled on the hem of his shirt and tugged it over his head, then used it to wipe the sweat from his neck.

Her tongue tripped at the sight of his naked, muscular torso. "Y-yes...job-hunting on the phone."

"Ah. If we had an opening at the gym, it would be yours."

She laughed. "I'm not exactly a walking billboard for a gym."

He skimmed her figure. "I disagree."

Her mouthful of lemonade when down the wrong way. She coughed violently.

"You okay there?" He patted her on the back.

"Yoo-hoo, Lin-da!"

She looked up to see Nan Boyd and the mob of neighborhood walking women on the sidewalk, arms pumping in tandem as they covered the ground like a swarm of colorful locusts. Necks stretched and mouths gawked at Stone, and Linda cringed inwardly, knowing how it must look. The rumor mill would be busy tonight. And if the women in the group she'd talked to this morning about a job had felt sorry for her, she was sure that was pretty much out the window.

"You should join us sometime!" Nan shouted.

"I will," she promised weakly.

When they were gone, Stone laughed. "I take it those are the community busybodies?"

"Yep."

"Sorry about that."

"I'll survive," she said, then took another drink from her glass. "This is so kind of you."

He shrugged his big shoulders, displacing lots of muscle. "It's not much."

"Well, it means a lot to me. I think Jarrod is still a little too young to wrestle with a lawnmower on this slope."

"Agreed. Consider me your lawn service for as long as you want me."

"That's very sweet, but I promise I won't take advantage of you."

He grinned. "Then the deal is totally off."

She smiled because she knew he was only teasing her. "Can I ask you a serious question?"

"Sure."

"The day you found Sullivan, did you notice a file anywhere around him?"

"You mean the file Klo is looking for?"

"Right."

"No, I didn't see anything like that."

"It couldn't have been under his jacket, or somehow wound up in the ambulance?"

"I don't see how."

"Okay, thanks. And I just want to say again how grateful I am that you acted so quickly."

He nodded. "You're welcome." He handed the empty glass back to her. "Guess I'd better get this done."

She walked back inside just as Octavia pulled up in the minivan. A few minutes later, she came in through the garage door.

"Hey," Linda said.

"Hey, yourself." Octavia pursed her mouth and looked at her expectantly. "What?"

"I see you have a new gardener."

"Stone is just being a good friend."

"Right...the man just wants to be friends."

"How was your day?"

"I so noticed you changed the subject there. Frustrating, thanks for asking." She shook her head. "I just feel like I have all the pieces where Richard's concerned, but I can't make them all fit."

Linda shrugged. "I'm pretty good at puzzles."

"No offense, but I'm a little brain dead now."

"So...just give me the big question you're trying to answer. Act like I know nothing about this case."

Octavia lifted her arms in a shrug. "Where can Richard be living in the area undetected—no credit card, no phone activity, nothing?"

"Someplace that takes only cash...or a hostel...or he broke into a home that's for sale...or he's staying at the YMCA."

"The cops checked the Y's, the homeless shelters, and the hostels. And the campgrounds, not that Richard would be caught dead camping. And we know from when they tried to pawn the art that they're out of cash."

"Unless they found a private collector to buy the art."

"No private collector is going to buy the art without papers and insurance. And if they went to a museum or a high end gallery, they would be reported immediately to the police. The people shady enough to do business on the black market aren't going to pay them very much."

"But they could barter the art for something that's more sellable, like jewelry."

"You're right...but if that's the case we'll never find them." She massaged her temples. "Okay, so what do you spend when you don't have credit or cash?"

"Stocks, bonds...gold?"

"We don't have any left," she said in a bleak voice. "Besides, the accounts would be flagged the minute he tried to make a transaction."

"How about some of the virtual currencies?"

"Good thought, but those transactions have to be backed by cash or credit cards."

Linda sighed. "Maybe I'm not good at this after all. Sorry—I'm not much of a world traveler. The last trip Sullivan and I took, we used points."

Octavia lifted her head. "What?"

"Well, if there's an upside of having credit cards maxed out, it's that you get a lot of travel points. So for our anniversary, we farmed out the kids and went to the Hyatt for the weekend."

Octavia bumped her palm to her forehead.

Linda squinted. "Are you okay?"

"Get in the van. I'm driving."

CHAPTER TWENTY-SEVEN

"I THINK WE should call the police," Linda said as they walked into the Marmot Hotel.

"No way," Octavia said. "First of all, we don't even know he's here. Second of all, if he is here, I want to talk to him before they do."

"He has a gun, sis."

"He's not going to shoot me."

She grabbed Octavia's arm. "You don't know what he's going to do. Let me call Oakley. He'll let you talk to Richard if he's here."

"Okay, if he's here, then you can call Oakley."

"Could he even check into the room without you?"

"Patsy has dark hair, everyone is always telling us how much we look alike. All they needed was my credit card number and something with my picture on it. And once they get in...everything is on points, nothing would be in his name. My credit card is maxed out, but there are lots of points to still be used."

They walked up to the reservations desk. "Guest Octavia Habersham?"

The clerk tapped on the keyboard, then looked up. "Do you want me to phone Ms. Habersham's room?"

She had to fight to remain calm. "Oh, no thanks—I'll call her on my cell to let her know I'm on my way."

"Very good, ma'am."

As they walked away, Linda was dialing Oakley.

"I don't feel well," Octavia said. "I'm going to find a restroom."

"I'll meet you right back here, and we'll wait for Oakley, okay?"

"Okay."

But as soon as she was out of earshot, she muttered, "Sorry, sis...this is something I have to do on my own."

She rode down to the basement and stepped off into a humid hallway. Then she used her cell phone to call the front desk of the hotel. "Yes, could you please deliver two extra towels to guest Octavia Habersham? Yes, right away. Thank you."

She disconnected the call and when she saw a maid coming out of laundry carrying two towels, she called the elevator car. They boarded together, and she let the maid choose a floor. Seventeen.

"That's my floor, too," she said.

When they reached the seventeenth floor, Octavia pretended to be busy in her purse until the maid alighted. She followed at a discreet distance until she could tell which room the woman was headed for.

"Are those towels for Habersham?"

The woman nodded.

"Those are for me," she said with a big smile. "Thank you so much." She slid a tip into the woman's hand, and waited until she'd walked away before facing the door.

With her heart in her throat, she knocked on the door. "Housekeeping," she said, disguising her voice. She stacked the towels in front of her face.

This was going to be so good.

But then the tip of a cold gun barrel was pressed against her temple. Octavia slid her gaze sideways to see the stocky blond man smiling at her. "I knew you'd lead me to him eventually."

The fact that he still had remnants of confetti glitter embedded in his skin was some consolation for knowing he was going to kill Richard.

And probably her, too, dammit.

The door opened—as usual, Richard had the worst timing. She got to enjoy a split second of gratification of sheer terror on his face when he saw it was her before being shoved inside. Glitter Guy shut the door behind them.

"Octavia!" Patsy cried. "Oh, my God, what is this?" She cowered behind Richard.

And great—they were both naked. Perfect. She would never be able to erase that picture from her mind. She pointed to Glitter Guy. "Ask him. He's the one with the gun."

"Shut up, everyone." He walked over to Richard and pointed the gun in his face. "Where is it?"

Richard went cross-eyed looking at the gun. "Where is what?"

"You know what. I'm going to count to three." He swung the gun until it pointed at Patsy's head. "One...two..."

"Richard, please!" begged Patsy. "Give him what he wants."

But Richard seemed oddly calm.

Then the guy swung the gun back to her. Octavia decided it was infinitely better to have a gun against your temple than to be staring down the barrel.

"One...two..."

"Wait!" Richard screamed. He held up his hands. "I'll get you what you want. Just don't kill my wife." Tears rolled down his face. "Please don't kill my wife."

Patsy's face went from outrage to fury when she realized the pecking order in the lineup. Octavia rolled her eyes. Didn't the idiot realize that by not being the love of Richard's life, she would probably live? Meanwhile, Richard had put a big, fat X on *her* ass if he didn't deliver.

"But I don't have it here," Richard said. "I gave it to someone for safekeeping."

"You mean the maid you were screwing? She's dead."

Richard went totally white. "Carla is...dead?"

"You were sleeping with your maid, too?" Patsy screamed.

"Shut up," the man said. "Richard, I talked to Carla before she died. She said she gave it back to you."

Octavia mentally retracted all the horrible things she'd ever said about Carla. The woman had protected her in the end.

Richard was shaking his head. She could tell his mind was racing over how he was going to get out of this.

A loud bang sounded on the door. "Police, open up!"

Octavia winced. This wasn't going to end well.

Meanwhile, her arms were tired of holding up the towels—her personal trainer would not be happy with her.

The man grabbed her in a choke hold, towels and all, and dragged her to the door. She could barely breathe.

"I'm coming out with a hostage," the man said. "Don't shoot and she lives."

"Open the door," he hissed into her ear.

She used her free hand to claw at the door handle. She turned it and slowly opened the door. On the other side of the threshold, Oakley Hall was holding a gun pointed at the man.

"Put the gun down and get back!" the man shouted.

Oakley did, slowly. As soon as the opening was big enough for both of them to fit through, the gunman half-pulled and half-dragged her down the hall to the elevator. When they got inside, he stabbed at the lobby button, then tightened his hold on her. "No little brats around to save you today."

"No," she croaked.

When the door opened, she made her move. She pretended to faint and went totally limp. She prayed he'd decide she was too cumbersome as a body shield and just leave her on the floor.

He did.

She opened her eyes in time to see him shot dead as soon as he stepped off the elevator.

When he fell, his face was turned toward her, his eyes open and vacant, the glitter on his skin macabre.

She scrambled up and was pulled off the elevator by the uniformed cop who'd killed the gunman. His badge read 'M. Jacobson.' "Are you alright, ma'am?"

She nodded, because her teeth were chattering now. She stepped over the body of the gunman and hung back until Oakley arrived with Richard and Patsy in tow, now dressed, and now in handcuffs. Richard looked like a broken man.

"Can I please talk to my wife before you take me away?" he asked.

Oakley looked to her for permission, and she nodded. The detective walked out of earshot with Patsy to give them some privacy.

"Listen to me, Octavia." Richard said. "I'm in deep with some really bad men. The only thing that can save me is a padded envelope I gave to Carla. Find that envelope. And when you do, don't tell anyone, don't trust anyone. This is bigger than you know. And the police are in on it, too." His eyes beseeched her. "I'm so, so sorry. Please don't hate me."

She opened her mouth to tell him she had the envelope, but Oakley was back.

"Time to go," he said.

"Remember what I said," Richard begged her.

"Octavia!"

She turned to see Linda running toward her. They embraced and Linda squeezed her tight. Octavia didn't want to ever let go.

Finally, Linda pulled back. "You took ten years off my life. Don't ever do something like that again." Then she smiled. "By yourself."

CHAPTER TWENTY-EIGHT

"SO UNCLE RICHARD is going to jail?" Maggie asked, fluffing up a white carnation made out of Kleenex tissue.

They were having a carnation-making party around the kitchen table with the remaining boxes of tissue.

"For the time being," Linda said.

"Will he see grandpa?" Jarrod asked.

Linda exchanged a glance with Octavia, and they both burst out laughing. What a family tree.

Linda twisted wire around a fan-folded tissue and handed it off to Jarrod. He tore off the edges so Octavia could pull the petals apart, and Maggie could do the final fluffing.

She watched Octavia interacting with her kids and her heart swelled. Only she knew how heartbroken and humiliated Octavia was by Richard's actions. A few nights since the arrest she had come to the kitchen for a late night drink of water and heard Octavia softly crying on the futon. Sometimes they would turn on the lights and talk over thawed chocolate-covered cherries, and sometimes she would crawl onto the battered futon and lie with her and both of them would cry for their husbands they had trusted to take care of them.

But Linda was determined to rebound. Oakley had pulled some strings and gotten her a clerical job in a bank. She was set to start in one week. It wasn't great money, but at least she wouldn't lose her home, and hopefully, it would lead to better opportunities.

She was grateful.

"The flowers are going to be pretty at the party," Maggie said. "Do you think we'll get them all done?"

"We still have two days," Linda said.

"Two more days of this?" Jarrod groaned.

She laughed. She'd decided to throw a closing party for the agency for the employees and their strip mall neighbors. It seemed like the best way to say goodbye to them...and to Octavia.

She would miss her when she returned to Louisville, but Linda knew it was time. Octavia had her own friends to get back to, and her life in Louisville to put back together. Richard was being held in a facility there, so when she moved back it would be easier for them to visit while he awaited trial.

She knew her sister hadn't yet decided what to do about her marriage, but she had let her know she was there for her no matter what she decided.

If anything positive had come out of the tragedies, it was that they were closer than they'd ever been. And although they were probably too polar opposite to ever be friends, they could be friendly sisters, and that was even better.

She caught Octavia's eye and they shared a smile.

———

Octavia handed off another carnation to Maggie. She would miss this the most, being gathered around the table. Linda was so lucky.

Maggie made a face. "I don't want you to leave, Aunt Tavey."

Octavia's heart bent toward the little girl.

"Aunt Tavey has to go back to her home," Linda said. "She has a lot to do."

Find a place to live, repair friendships, get a job, deal with my marriage.

"I'll come back to visit," she promised.

And there was still the matter of the envelope that Grim was holding for her. She hadn't shared with him—or anyone—what Richard had told her, and still hadn't decided what she was going to do.

"People always say they'll visit," Maggie groused. "But they never do."

"I will," Octavia said. Then she got up and went to the den, returning with two boxes. "I got you each a goodbye gift."

"That wasn't necessary," Linda murmured.

"It was for me," Octavia said.

"I love presents," Maggie said, clapping her hands.

"Can we open them?" Jarrod asked.

She nodded.

"Me first!" said Maggie. The look on her face when she opened the box was worth gold. "Pom poms!" She squealed and jumped up and down in the chair.

"Those are my UK cheerleader pom poms," Octavia said. "I'm entrusting them to you now."

"I will love them," Maggie said, nuzzling the blue and white fringes to her face.

She leaped down to throw her arms around Octavia's neck. "I love you, Aunt Tavey."

Octavia's heart billowed. "I love you, too, sweetie."

"Now me?" Jarrod asked.

She nodded.

He opened the long slender box and grinned. "Drumsticks! These are cool."

"And they go with the set of drums that Grim is holding for you at the pawn shop."

His whole face lit up. "For real?"

"For real."

"Okay, that really wasn't necessary," Linda said, sending lasers across the table.

"I'll be gone," Octavia said sweetly. She got a hug from Jarrod, too, and he hung on longer than she thought he would.

"I'll miss you," he said.

"I'll miss you, too. I expect to hear a drum solo when I come back."

Her phone rang and she was surprised to see Dunk Duncan's name come up. "This is Dunk," she said to Linda. "Let me take this."

"Make sure he's coming by the night of the party to get the library."

"Okay."

She walked into the next room and connected the call. "Hello?"

"Hi, Octavia. It's Dunk."

What a voice...the man was lethal. "Hey, Dunk. What's up?"

"Actually, I'm calling with a job offer."

She frowned. "To do what?"

"To come and work for me."

Surprise barbed through her...followed by excitement. She'd enjoyed the investigative work, but hadn't considered doing it for a living. But as soon as the possibility wound its way into her head, the idea began to bloom.

"I'm listening."

CHAPTER TWENTY-NINE

LINDA DUCKED under a clump of white paper carnations, and walked into Sullivan's office to take a breather from the crowd. All the business neighbors had shown up, with some extras. The young waitress from the Waffle House had stopped by...she had taken a special interest in Maggie and Jarrod, which Linda appreciated.

Klo was there, of course, and Stone. They were always good company. Grim was there and Linda watched him watch her sister....there was something going on there that she couldn't put her finger on. It wasn't an affair—in fact, it was almost the opposite. The two of them seemed to enjoy a shared animosity toward each other. It was....strange.

Maria Munoza was there, although she stayed on the fringes of the conversations. The woman was nothing if not mysterious.

Dunk Duncan had arrived and although he'd said he would "take the library off their hands," it was clear he was there to see Octavia. It was probably the only good thing about Octavia leaving Lexington, Linda thought, because she was afraid if Octavia stayed, another marriage might be compromised. And Dunk seemed like the kind of man who would never leave his wife.

She turned a small circle around Sullivan's office. Closing his agency felt like burying him all over again...he'd had such high hopes for building something for his family.

But even the ficus tree next to the window had died, which seemed like a sign.

The new tenant had already mounted a big sign over the storefront. Klo didn't know who was taking over, just that they would be moving in tomorrow.

The sign was covered with a white tarp, but if its size was any indication of the new owner's plans, then the business was sure to be a success.

"Why are you hiding in here?"

She turned to see Oakley at the door. She smiled. "I'm not hiding...just thinking...remembering. Thank you for coming." She gave him an impulsive hug.

His hand was warm on her back, his embrace comforting and just so... good.

She pulled back. "And thank you for my new job."

He beamed. "Glad to help."

The door opened and Octavia's face appeared. "Linda, can you guys come outside, I have an announcement to make."

"Sounds very intriguing," Linda said.

They all crowded out onto the sidewalk below the big sign. It was still daylight, with customers coming and going from the other businesses. They attracted attention as Octavia passed out champagne flutes. A few passersby wandered down.

"Do you know what's going on?" Oakley whispered.

"I have no idea."

His hand hovered at the small of her back, and it wasn't unwelcome.

"Everyone," Octavia said, "I have an announcement to make about a new job."

Linda blinked in surprise.

"Dunk, can you come up to help me with this?"

The tall man moved to stand next to her, his body language proprietary. Whatever the announcement was, he seemed in on it...and that made Linda nervous.

Octavia lifted her glass. "I'd like everyone to join me in toasting a new venture in investigative work."

Linda frowned. Where was this going?

Octavia grabbed a tie around one end of the covered sign. "Dunk, will you get the other end?"

Dunk's expression changed from smug to confused, like the rest of them. Linda realized that whatever had just happened, it was not what he had planned. But he went along.

"On three," she said. "One, two, three." They yanked the ties at the same time and the tarp fell to reveal TWO GUYS DETECTIVE AGENCY.

"My sister Linda and I are going to have our own investigative agency!"

"What?" Dunk said.

"What?" Oakley said.

"What?" Linda said. She looked at Octavia, utterly confused.

But everyone else cheered and lifted their glasses in a happy salute. Octavia came running over to Linda. "What do you think, sis?"

Linda finally found her voice. "I...I...I think you should've asked me first."

Octavia's smile dimmed. "I was afraid you would talk me out of it. I thought it would be better if I tried to talk you *into* it." Then her animation returned. "With my marketing know-how and your connections to the police department—"

"Wait a minute. Oakley isn't my personal connection." Indeed, standing a few feet away, he did not look pleased at the prospect of them starting their own agency. Her mind reeled. She and Octavia couldn't work together side by side, long term—they were too different. "And besides, I'm starting a new job in a few days."

"A *boring* job," Octavia said. "Is that what you want to do day in and day out, work at a bank? Handle other people's money, when we could be making our own money, and building a business together?"

Linda shook her head. "I just don't think this is going to work. I'm sorry."

Octavia's shoulders fell in disappointment, but she nodded. "I'm sorry, too."

"It's a beautiful sign, though. And it looks expensive."

"It was."

Linda frowned. "How did you pay for it?"

Octavia didn't answer, but her hand floated to her neck for a split second, and Linda realized she wasn't wearing her jewelry...and hadn't been for a couple of days.

"You sold your jewelry to pay for this sign?"

Octavia lifted her hands. "What can I say? I'm all in."

Linda's heart expanded. If her sister was so committed to the joint venture, the least she could do was try. "Then so am I."

Octavia's face lit up. "Really?"

Linda nodded, then pulled her into a hug. "I didn't want to go work in a bank anyway."

They laughed, then clinked their glasses together.

"To sisterhood," Octavia said.

Linda smiled. "I'll drink to that."

-The End-

**Don't miss the next book in the
TWO GUYS DETECTIVE AGENCY series, coming late 2013!**

A NOTE FROM THE AUTHOR

Thank you so very much for taking the time to read the first book in my new mystery series TWO GUYS DETECTIVE AGENCY! I so hope you enjoyed it. I'm thrilled to be writing a P.I. series, which I've wanted to do since I took the coursework to become a private investigator 15 years ago. (I received a 95% on my shooting range exam.) And I'm happy to be setting the story in my old stomping grounds of Lexington, Kentucky, where I worked for many years and still have close ties. Since I'll be living vicariously through Linda and Octavia, I'm planning many more adventures for them, and I hope you'll come along.

If you enjoyed TWO GUYS DETECTIVE AGENCY and feel inclined to leave an Amazon review, I would appreciate it very much!

And are you signed up to receive notices of my future book releases? If not, please visit www.stephaniebond.com to join my email list. I will never share or sell your address. And you can unsubscribe at any time.

Thanks again for your time and interest, and for telling your friends about my books. If you'd like to know more about some of my other books, please scroll ahead to the next section.

Happy reading!
Stephanie Bond

OTHER WORKS BY STEPHANIE BOND

Humorous romantic mysteries:

TWO GUYS DETECTIVE AGENCY—*Even Victoria can't keep a secret from us...*
OUR HUSBAND—*Hell hath no fury like three women scorned!*
KILL THE COMPETITION—*There's only one sure way to the top.*
GOT YOUR NUMBER—*You can run, but your past will eventually catch up with you.*
PARTY CRASHERS—*No invitation, no alibi.*
WHOLE LOTTA TROUBLE—*They didn't plan on getting caught...*
IN DEEP VOODOO—*A woman stabs a voodoo doll of her ex, and then he's found murdered!*
VOODOO OR DIE—*Another voodoo doll, another untimely demise...*
6 ½ BODY PARTS—*a BODY MOVERS series novella*
BUMP IN THE NIGHT—*a short mystery*

Romances:

ALMOST A FAMILY—*Fate gave them a second chance at love...*
LICENSE TO THRILL—*She's between a rock and a hard body...*
STOP THE WEDDING!—*If anyone objects to this wedding, speak now...*
THREE WISHES—*Be careful what you wish for!*
THE ARRANGEMENT—*Friends become lovers...what could possibly go wrong?*

Nonfiction:

GET A LIFE! 8 STEPS TO CREATE YOUR OWN LIFE LIST—*a short how-to for mapping out your personal life list!*

13

CPSIA information can be obtained at www.ICGtesting.com
Printed in the USA
LVOW12s2008170615

442844LV00005B/231/P